D0117747

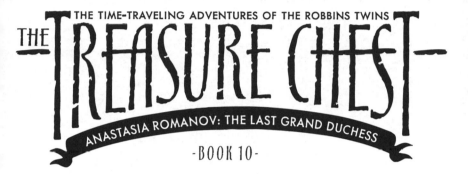

THE TIME-TRAVELING ADVENTURES OF THE ROBBINS TWINS

THE TREASURE CHEST

ANASTASIA ROMANOV: THE LAST GRAND DUCHESS

-BOOK 10-

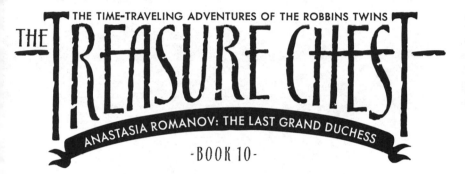

THE TIME-TRAVELING ADVENTURES OF THE ROBBINS TWINS

THE TREASURE CHEST

ANASTASIA ROMANOV: THE LAST GRAND DUCHESS

-BOOK 10-

BY *NEW YORK TIMES* BEST-SELLING AUTHOR

ANN HOOD

Grosset & Dunlap
An Imprint of Penguin Group (USA) LLC

GROSSET & DUNLAP
Published by the Penguin Group
Penguin Group (USA) LLC, 375 Hudson Street, New York, New York 10014, USA

USA | Canada | UK | Ireland | Australia | New Zealand | India | South Africa | China

penguin.com
A Penguin Random House Company

Library of Congress Cataloging-in-Publication Data is available.

Design by Giuseppe Castellano.
Map illustration by Giuseppe Castellano and © 2013 by Penguin Group (USA) LLC.

ISBN 978-0-448-46771-9 (pbk)   10 9 8 7 6 5 4 3 2 1
ISBN 978-0-448-46770-2 (hc)   10 9 8 7 6 5 4 3 2 1

To everyone at Penguin who helped to make The Treasure Chest come to life: Don, Jen, Jordan, Giuseppe, Jed, Carmela, Elyse, Emily, Karl, Max, Nico, Felicia, Samantha, Adam, Meagan. And of course, Francesco.

CHAPTER ONE

THE ZIFF TWINS DEPART

Great-Uncle Thorne smiled at Maisie and Felix, his blue eyes twinkling in a way they had never seen before. He actually looked, Maisie realized with surprise, happy.

"My only regret," Great-Uncle Thorne said, "is that I cannot go with you."

"Go?" Felix asked, immediately anxious. "Go where?"

Great-Uncle Thorne's smile widened.

"Why, to Imperial Russia," he said, surprising Maisie once again. Ordinarily, he would have called Felix a dolt for not figuring out what always seemed so obvious to Great-Uncle Thorne, and so *not* obvious to Maisie and her brother.

"Is that different from regular Russia?" Hadley asked.

The Ziff twins, having delivered the message from Amy Pickworth, still sat together on the love seat, waiting for further instructions.

Great-Uncle Thorne shook his head sadly.

"What has happened to education?" he asked, his gaze sweeping up to the ceiling as if he might find an answer there. "My sister and I were taught right here at Elm Medona by brilliant tutors. Latin. French. The classics. And, of course, history."

He chuckled, still staring at the ceiling and its twinkling white lights.

"Our history teacher was a Yale man, Mr. Franklin Smith. Of course, he let Maisie and me call him Smitty. Got a kick out of that, actually. Smitty appeared every morning at eleven, vaguely disheveled but always with his Yale tie and a straw boater."

"A straw boat?" Maisie asked, but Great-Uncle Thorne ignored her.

"Up to the Map Room he'd march us—"

"The Map Room?" Maisie interrupted.

She had poked in every corner of Elm Medona. She'd opened closets and stepped inside. She'd stood in many of the rooms that never got used and whose names no one seemed to know. Of course she'd been surprised by the Fairy Room, but it was secret, hidden.

"There's no Map Room in Elm Medona," Maisie said certainly.

Now Great-Uncle Thorne frowned at her.

"Of course there's a Map Room. And you and your coterie should obviously spend some time in it. If you did, you would know that Imperial Russia was so enormous that when it was night in the west, it was dawn on the Pacific. And that the land that stretched between made up one-sixth of all the land in the world. And that land was ruled by one man. The Tsar of Imperial Russia."

"Show us," Felix said, his mind already trying to conjure such an immense country. "Take us to the Map Room and show us."

Great-Uncle Thorne considered Felix's request. The children, their eyes on him, waited hopefully.

"I suppose if you're going there, you should understand a bit about what you're getting into," he said thoughtfully.

"Getting into?" Felix repeated. "You mean it's dangerous there?"

Great-Uncle Thorne shrugged.

"Actually, Maisie and I never had the pleasure of visiting Imperial Russia. It is the one place that our father warned us against. Of course, I'm sure that was because of what happened there in 1918 . . ."

He paused.

"If we couldn't get back here and got stuck with the family . . ."

He paused again.

Maisie and Felix sneaked a glance at each other.

"Not to worry!" Great-Uncle Thorne said finally, with too much bravado. "You'll get back without a hitch. Why wouldn't you?"

"Why wouldn't we?" Maisie asked. "Why did Phinneas Pickworth fear you and Great-Aunt Maisie wouldn't be able to return?"

Great-Uncle Thorne's face softened. "I believe it was just the love of a father for his children," he said softly.

Before Maisie could question Great-Uncle Thorne further, her mother's voice interrupted.

"What is this?" she said, stepping into the Fairy Room, awestruck.

She bent and touched the grass that covered the floor.

"Why, this grass is *real*!" she declared.

Her eyes tried to take it all in: the walls covered with ivy and pink and blue morning glories, the angel hair and twinkling lights on the ceiling.

"Jennifer," Great-Uncle Thorne said firmly, "this was my mother's most private place. It's not for . . . general consumption."

"But who tends all these flowers and grass?"

"There's a special employee of Elm Medona whose sole purpose is to maintain this room," Great-Uncle Thorne answered. "But you have to leave it, I'm afraid. As I said, it's—"

"Yes," their mother replied, "not for general consumption. But then why are the children in here? And the Ziff twins?"

No one had an answer.

Quiet fell over the Fairy Room.

Maisie and Felix's mother let out a big sigh. "Sometimes," she said, "I feel like something strange is going on around here."

"It is," Great-Uncle Thorne said. "Your children frequently time travel and meet famous people when those people were children."

Maisie and Felix both gasped.

But their mother laughed. Hard. "That's a good one," she said.

She wiped the corners of her eyes, shaking her head. "Maybe I'll go along with you next time," she added.

"Sorry," Great-Uncle Thorne said. "You have to be a twin."

"Oh! I see!" Her eyes settled on the Ziff twins. "Well, then, take Hadley and Rayne along with you!"

The children all forced a laugh.

If she only knew, Felix thought as his mother told them breakfast was ready and they needed to get ready for school. *If she only knew.*

❄

Maisie had thought that landing the lead in *The Crucible* would skyrocket her into popularity. But nothing seemed to change. Instead, Hadley remained her only friend. Unless she counted Jim Duncan, who was really Felix's friend but at least seemed to like her, too.

But today, even Hadley seemed to be ignoring her. Maybe Great-Uncle Thorne and Imperial Russia had upset her. Maybe Hadley didn't want anything to do with The Treasure Chest and fancy Fabergé eggs made by the Imperial jeweler for the Tsar. Or, Maisie thought as she unsuccessfully tried to get Hadley's attention during social studies, maybe Hadley didn't want anything more to do with her.

"Entire countries have vanished," Mrs. Witherspoon was saying. "Through war or independence or colonization or crumbling governments, borders shift. Names change. Rulers get deposed."

She pulled down one of the maps that hung over the blackboard.

"Abyssinia, for example," Mrs. Witherspoon said, pointing to somewhere in Africa. "Abyssinia was an empire for more than eight hundred years, an empire that spanned present-day Ethiopia, Eritrea, Djibouti, parts of northern Somalia, southern Egypt, eastern Sudan . . ."

Her long pointer tapped each area on the map as she spoke. *Tap. Tap. Tap.*

Maisie willed Hadley to turn around so she could roll her eyes and make her laugh. But Hadley appeared to be completely engrossed in Abyssinia.

"In 1974, the monarchy was overthrown in a

coup d'état," Mrs. Witherspoon continued, "and Abyssinia ceased to exist."

Mrs. Witherspoon went on talking about Rhodesia and the Belgian Congo. She pulled down another map, this one of Europe, and tapped and pointed and talked about Austria-Hungary and East Germany, but all Maisie could think about was why Hadley Ziff was ignoring her.

More maps, more pointing. Ceylon and Persia and Siam.

Maisie ripped a piece of notebook paper from her social studies notebook and rolled it into a tight ball.

She narrowed her eyes for better aim and lobbed the ball at the back of Hadley's head.

A direct hit!

Hadley's hand shot up and retrieved the paper from where it landed between her back and her chair. But she did not turn around.

Mrs. Witherspoon kept talking about overthrown monarchies and revolutions.

Maisie tore another sheet of paper from her notebook. This time she wrote a note on it: *A be sinny ya at lunch!*

A clever pun, Maisie decided. Taking the word

Abyssinia and making it sound like *I'll be seeing ya!* Surely Hadley would appreciate that.

Maisie folded the note into a little paper airplane and sent it flying so that it would land somewhere near Hadley's feet.

Bull's-eye!

Instead of picking it up, Hadley twisted her head around and glared at Maisie.

Maisie began reviewing the morning in the Fairy Room. What had she done to make Hadley angry with her? Hadley and Rayne had not taken her mother's invitation to stay for breakfast. Was that another clue? They'd given a good reason, telling everyone that their parents were waiting for them at the Kozy Kitchen for a family breakfast. Had that just been an excuse?

"Do tell us all where you are, Miss Robbins," Mrs. Witherspoon said, her voice interrupting Maisie's thoughts.

"Um," Maisie said, squinting at the map. What had she missed? What was Mrs. Witherspoon talking about now?

"Can someone tell Maisie what our reports are on?" Mrs. Witherspoon asked the class. "Hadley?"

Reluctantly, Hadley stood. Even though she turned toward Maisie, her eyes stayed on the scratched linoleum floor.

"A country that's disappeared?" she said.

"And?" Mrs. Witherspoon prompted.

"And what it was like before and what happened and what country it is now," Hadley finished and sat right back down.

"Did you get all that, Maisie?" Mrs. Witherspoon asked.

Maisie stared hard at Hadley's back, at her tangle of dark hair.

"Maisie!" Mrs. Witherspoon said.

Maisie looked at Mrs. Witherspoon, and then at the map hanging in front of the blackboard.

"I already know what I'm doing my report on," she said.

"Oh, do you?" Mrs. Witherspoon said, peering at Maisie over the top of her glasses.

"Imperial Russia," Maisie said.

At that, Hadley *did* turn around.

Maisie grinned. "Imperial Russia was so enormous," she said, "that when it was night in the west, it was dawn on the Pacific. And the land that stretched between made up one-sixth of all the land in the world. And that land was ruled by one man. The Tsar."

Mrs. Witherspoon looked impressed.

Hadley looked upset.

"Well," Mrs. Witherspoon said, "I had no idea you were interested in Russian history."

"Oh yes," Maisie said. "I'd even like to go there sometime."

Hadley turned back around and dropped her head.

What is wrong with Hadley? Maisie wondered.

"I look forward to your report," Mrs. Witherspoon said.

But Maisie wasn't listening anymore. Instead, she was plotting how to make sure Hadley didn't get away when the lunch bell rang. Hadley wasn't angry with her, Maisie realized; she was upset about The Treasure Chest.

The bell rang, and even though Maisie was waiting, ready to leap out of her seat and get to Hadley, she was stopped by Alex Andropov, arguably the smartest kid at Anne Hutchinson Elementary School.

"Maisie," Alex said, pushing his glasses up the bridge of his nose. They slid right back down to the tip. "I had no idea."

How could it be that some kids—like Felix—looked cool in glasses, Maisie wondered, and other kids—like Alex Andropov—looked nerdy? The fact that Alex cut his hair too short for his round face and often wore white shirts with puffy sleeves that he insisted were called poet's shirts didn't help. Plus, he was skinny and pale and often was absent for weeks at a time. Although to some kids this made him mysterious and provoked speculation that he was the son of a billionaire and traveled the world with his father, to Maisie his absences just made her forget him until he showed up in class again.

Maisie peered over his head and watched Hadley approach the exit door.

"No idea about what?" Maisie asked impatiently. She wanted to push past him, but he had positioned himself in such a way that he had her trapped.

"Your interest in the Russian Empire!" Alex said.

"Huh? Oh right. Imperial Russia."

She craned her neck. Hadley was gone.

"I'm Russian," Alex was saying proudly. "And I'm

a direct descendant of the Romanovs."

Maisie frowned. "Who?"

She moved forward, even though it meant wedging herself between Alex and her desk.

Alex's face fell with disappointment. "How can you be a student of Imperial Russia and not know the Romanovs?"

"I'm a new student," Maisie said. "Alex, can we talk about this later? I have to go."

With that his face brightened again.

"Today? After school?"

"Sure," Maisie said, and worked her way free of Alex Andropov.

The classroom had emptied out. Even Mrs. Witherspoon was gone. Maisie picked up her pace and hurried down the corridor to the lunchroom.

As soon as Maisie walked in the noisy, crowded room, the smell of Taco Day hit her. It looked like the entire school was lined up at the taco bar, piling ground beef, bright orange shredded cheese, chopped tomatoes, and ribbons of tired lettuce into taco shells.

Everyone except Felix, Rayne, and Hadley.

They sat at a table, leaning in close to one another.

And Hadley and Rayne were both crying.

"What's going on?" Maisie said after she pushed her way through the lines at the taco bar to get to them.

She didn't wait for an answer.

"I've been trying to get your attention all morning," she told Hadley.

"I know," Hadley said, sniffling. "I couldn't tell you in class."

"Tell me what?" Maisie demanded, her frustration growing even more.

"We're moving," Rayne said, also sniffling. "To Buenos Aires."

"But you can't!" Maisie said. "You're my best friend," she said, again to Hadley. She could have added *my only friend* and it would have been true.

"You're *my* best friend," Hadley said.

"And now we won't get to find out what happens in Russia," Rayne said.

"Of course you can," Felix jumped in. "We'll go to The Treasure Chest right after school."

Hadley and Rayne shook their heads.

"A car is picking us up at three o'clock and taking us directly to the airport," Rayne said.

"That's how it works when your father's in the CIA," Hadley added. "We never get a heads-up on where or *when* we're going next."

Maisie couldn't do anything to stop it, she realized. She put her arm around Hadley's shoulders and bent her tangled dirty-blond hair until it touched Hadley's dark curly hair. They were opposites of each other physically. But inside . . . Inside they were like twins. Maisie got a whiff of her friend's mint shampoo. Then she started to cry, too.

CHAPTER TWO

ALEX ANDROPOV

Maisie and Felix stood outside on the steps of Anne Hutchinson Elementary School and watched as a big black sedan took Hadley and Rayne Ziff away from them.

Behind them, the door burst open, but neither of them turned around.

"There you are!" someone shouted.

Felix glanced up.

"Hi, Alex," he said glumly.

Alex stood beside Maisie and peered in the same direction where her eyes were focused.

The big black sedan was just a tiny dot down the road.

"How about coming to my house?" Alex asked.

"I can show you some really cool stuff from Russia."

"Can I take a rain check?" Maisie asked as the tiny dot disappeared from sight.

"I guess," Alex said sadly.

"I'll come tomorrow," Maisie said. What was he all sad about? She was the one who had just lost her best friend.

"Don't you have *Crucible* rehearsals tomorrow?" Felix reminded her.

"The next day, then," Maisie said. "The report isn't even due for two weeks."

"It's just that I called my grandmother and told her you were coming, and she's making *pirozhki*."

"I don't know what that is," Maisie mumbled, wondering how she had gotten herself into this predicament in the first place.

"And *blini*," Alex continued. He added, "Traditional food of Russia."

Maisie sighed.

"You're Russian?" Felix asked politely.

Alex nodded. "I'm a direct descendant of the Romanovs."

"And they're . . . famous Russians?" Felix asked.

"The royal family!" Alex said.

"Like the Tsar?" Felix asked.

When Alex nodded, Felix grinned.

"Maisie," Felix said, "I think it would be a good idea for both of us to go to Alex's house today."

Maisie glowered at her brother. All she wanted to do was go home, climb into bed, and feel bad.

"In case we ever, you know," Felix said, staring at her hard, "go to Russia."

Maisie could practically hear Great-Uncle Thorne reprimanding them for being unprepared, for using The Treasure Chest all willy-nilly. This time, it seemed very important to actually be prepared. Hadn't Great-Uncle Thorne said Phinneas Pickworth wouldn't even allow him and Great-Aunt Maisie to go to Imperial Russia? Hadn't he said it was unsafe?

Felix and Alex were both waiting for her to say something.

"Why are we just standing here?" Maisie asked them. "Let's go!"

Alex Andropov lived in a dark red Colonial house on Spring Street with a plaque beside the front door that read:

THE LLOYD EDWARD HOUSE
BUILT 1792

"Wow!" Felix said. "Your house is really old."

But Alex waved his hand as if that didn't interest him.

"This whole street is full of houses built during the Colonial days," he said. "Down there, the White Horse Tavern is even older; 16-something."

Maisie and Felix stole a glance at each other. They were impressed. But clearly Alex wasn't. He jiggled a large key in the lock of the blue front door until it finally slipped into place. Then he turned it, and the door creaked open.

"Tsarist Russia goes back to 1533," Alex said as he stepped inside and motioned for Maisie and Felix to follow. "But Russia goes back to around 862."

They were standing in a small foyer with an umbrella stand filled with umbrellas, and a steep crooked stairway. On either side of the foyer there was a pale green door open to a room.

Felix wrinkled his nose. The house smelled strongly of cabbage.

But Alex smiled. "I smell *pirozhki*."

"Great," Felix said, trying his best to sound enthusiastic.

Alex wasn't taking note of either of them. Instead

he bounded into the room at the right, calling, "Babushka!"

Maisie and Felix followed him. The room had heavy maroon drapes tied with thick gold braided rope that ended in fat tassels, and a thick Oriental rug over wide floorboards. The furniture looked too big for the small room, and they had to squeeze past some of it to keep up with Alex, who hadn't even paused. He continued through the next room, which was only slightly larger but also full of oversize furniture. A long dining-room table dominated the room, and a dozen throne-like chairs crowded around it. Maisie paused to study the walls, which were painted with a mural that depicted life in a foreign country, probably long ago.

When Alex realized she wasn't behind him, he peered around the corner.

"Moscow," he said, pointing to one wall. "St. Petersburg, Crimea," he said, pointing to two other walls.

The fireplace was so tall that there was only a sliver of wall above it, and that had a coat of arms painted on it.

Alex disappeared and Maisie went after him.

She stepped into a small kitchen. *The source of that cabbage*, she thought.

A plump woman with a wrinkled face, bright blue eyes, and gray braids peeking out from beneath a colorful kerchief smiled a toothless smile at the three children.

Felix heard Alex say: *"Babushka, vstrechayus' druz'yami."*

Instinctively, Maisie's hand went to the shard hanging around her neck on a piece of yarn. That shard had let her understand and be understood in languages from Tagalog to Italian. She had forgotten to take it off last night, and now she could understand and be understood . . . in Russian.

So Maisie heard Alex say: "Grandmother, meet my friends."

"Nice to meet you," Maisie said, remembering her manners for once. "I'm Maisie Robbins."

Alex gaped at her.

"You speak Russian?" he gasped.

"Um," she said. "Just a little."

Alex's grandmother was hugging her and telling her how well she spoke the mother tongue.

Felix, who had taken his piece of the shard off

and put it carefully away in his underwear drawer, shook his head. How weird was it that Maisie spoke Russian? Alex could tell the whole school, and then what?

"In fact," Maisie was saying, "that's about all I can say. I learned how to say that same phrase in lots of languages back in first grade."

Alex narrowed his eyes behind his glasses.

"Can you guys say it in Swedish?" he asked her. "And what other languages? Dutch? German?"

Maisie laughed nervously. "We've forgotten most of it, I guess."

Babushka released Maisie long enough to hoist an enormous silver platter of food onto her own shoulder and waddle out to the dining room.

"*Davayte yest*," Alex said, keeping his eyes on Maisie, who understood perfectly that he'd said, "Let's eat." But she just laughed and shrugged.

"Let's eat," Alex said.

"That I understand," Maisie said.

Although Felix didn't like the cabbage-stuffed *pirozhki*, the *blini* reminded him of crepes. They were stuffed with mild cheese and topped with black cherries in thick syrup. He filled his plate with those, and sat at the big dining-room table, which was covered with a white tablecloth complete with a heavy ornate silver candelabra. The house seemed Old World somehow, as if they had traveled back to a fancier, more formal time. But this wasn't time traveling. This was just Alex and his babushka, a woman who had left Russia long ago.

Alex translated everything his grandmother said, adding his own details. Even though Maisie could understand the Russian, she was careful to pretend she couldn't, and she nodded only after Alex spoke. Still, she thought Alex watched her a little too closely so she tried her hardest to keep her face blank.

Apparently, the last Tsar, Nicholas, had not wanted to become Tsar.

"In fact," Alex told them, "he was third in line. But his oldest brother died young, and his next-older brother suffered from tuberculosis and was not fit to rule."

When his father died suddenly, Nicholas had no choice but to take over what he referred to as the job he'd feared his entire life. He hastily married Alexandra, a German duchess who was distrusted by the Russians.

"Some say she was just shy," Alex translated, "but

most thought she was cold and looked down on the Russians, like she was better than them. Of course," he added on his own, "she did provide an heir. Not that it mattered."

Maisie chewed her bottom lip. *What terrible thing happened to the Tsar and his family?* It was something bad enough for Phinneas Pickworth to worry about his children going to Imperial Russia.

"So Nicholas and Alexandra had a son?" Felix asked. "Why didn't he want to become Tsar after his father?"

Alex quickly translated Felix's question for his grandmother.

Her face creased with sadness, and she dabbed at her eyes with a lace-edged handkerchief.

Babushka shook her head and spoke for some time before Alex interpreted.

"They actually had five children," he said. "In Russia, back then, when the Empress had a baby, everyone waited to count the number of shots from the cannon at Peter and Paul Fortress in St. Petersburg. One hundred and one shots from the cannon meant a girl was born. That happened four times."

"Oh!" Felix said between chews of another *blini*. "So they had four daughters?"

"Olga, Tatiana, Maria, and Anastasia," Alex said. "And then, in 1904, the cannon boomed three hundred times."

"A boy," Maisie said.

Alex nodded. "His Imperial Highness Alexei Nikolaevich, Sovereign Heir Tsarevich, Grand Duke of Russia."

"Phew!" Maisie said, letting out a long whistle. "That's a mouthful."

"Better known as Alexei—" Alex began, but his grandmother interrupted him.

He listened and nodded.

"After the second Tsar, Alexei, the Gentle," he translated for her.

He added, "How ironic."

Maisie waited for more of an explanation, but Alex was once again listening to his grandmother.

"When the Tsarevich would appear in public, the people of Russia went wild. Of course they wanted to glimpse him, especially because he was kept at home most of the time," Alex finally said.

"To protect him?" Felix asked.

Alex glanced over at Maisie. "You are interested in Imperial Russia," he said. "Why don't you explain to Felix?"

"Explain?" Maisie stalled.

"Tell him why the Tsarevich was overprotected," Alex prodded.

"Because he was . . . the Tsarevich . . . ," Maisie stammered.

"I don't know why you say you have a fascination with Russia when you don't know anything about it!" Alex said, laughing.

He turned serious as soon as Babushka shot him a warning look. Alex apologized to her in Russian, explaining what he was laughing at.

But he quickly turned serious when he told Maisie and Felix why the Tsarevich was so overprotected.

"Hemophilia," he said, his voice somber.

"A blood disease?" Felix guessed. They'd had *hemo* on a prefix quiz last week.

Alex nodded. "A genetic one, passed on through females. His mother was a carrier."

"What does it do?" Maisie asked. "This hemo—"

"Hemophilia," Alex said again. "It's a rare

bleeding disorder that prevents the blood from clotting properly."

"You mean if he got a scratch or cut, his blood wouldn't clot?" Maisie asked.

"And he'd bleed to death?" Felix added, horrified.

"Minor things like that wouldn't kill him, no. But bruises, joint injuries, that kind of thing can cause internal bleeding, terrible pain, and sometimes even death."

"You really are an expert on everything," Felix said admiringly.

Alex's face turned grim.

"Sadly, in this case that's true, Felix," he said. "You see, I'm an expert on hemophilia because I have it, too."

Felix gaped at Alex. How could a kid from school have something so serious?

"I know. It's weird," Alex said as if he'd read Felix's mind.

Embarrassed, Felix mumbled, "No, no . . ."

"Ironically," Alex said ruefully, "hemophilia is called the royal disease. Queen Victoria was a carrier."

"Why do you say 'ironically,' Alex?" Maisie

asked, loving that Alex used such a big word, even though it had been on their literary-terms vocabulary quiz just last week.

"Poor Alexei," Alex said, shaking his head sadly. "He suffered so much and all because of his bloodline. That's why he had hemophilia. And that's why what happened to him and his family happened, because they were royalty."

"Do you suffer?" Felix asked Alex. "A lot?"

Alex looked tenderly to his grandmother. "The worst part is how much it worries Babushka when I have an incident." He grimaced. "That's what we call them around here. Incidents. In truth, they're hemorrhages. Painful. Terrifying."

"Alex?" Maisie said, her voice low. "What happened to the Tsarevich? I know it was something terrible."

Alex told his grandmother what Maisie was asking.

Babushka sighed, then nodded at Alex.

"He was murdered," Alex said. "Along with his entire family."

Felix gasped. "Murdered!"

"After the Revolution of 1917. The family was

taken prisoner by the Bolsheviks, held at Ekaterinburg, and murdered."

"All the sisters, too?" Maisie asked.

Alex translated Maisie's question for his grandmother, who nodded solemnly.

Dabbing at the corners of her eyes, Babushka said, *"Oni dazhe ubil sobaku."*

Maisie, who had forgotten her ruse that she couldn't understand Russian, blurted in Russian before Alex had the chance to translate, "Why would they kill the dog?"

Felix's mind was so full of questions that he didn't even notice Maisie speaking in Russian. All he could think about was who these Bolsheviks were. Why was there a revolution? Why would anyone kill an entire family? Was this what Phinneas Pickworth worried about? That somehow Thorne and Maisie would be in Russia in 1917 and be held prisoners with the family?

The silence forced Felix back to reality.

Alex stared at Maisie for what seemed a very long time.

"Luchshe sprosit, pochemu vy govorite na russkom yazyke?" he said finally, not taking his eyes off Maisie.

CHAPTER THREE

FABERGÉ

"I couldn't help it!" Maisie insisted as she and Felix headed back to Elm Medona from Alex's house. "Hearing about a whole family getting murdered kind of upset me, okay?"

Even after Alex had asked Maisie: *Luchshe sprosit, pochemu vy govorite na russkom yazyke?* (which meant: *A better question is why do you speak Russian?*), Maisie had tried to pretend that she didn't speak Russian.

"What a disaster," Felix moaned as they turned onto Memorial Boulevard.

"Big deal," Maisie said. "So he thinks I know a little Russian."

"A little?" Felix said. "You understood Babushka and then you responded to what she said. That's not a little. That's actually speaking Russian."

"Who cares, though?" Maisie said. "Alex Andropov isn't going to tell anybody, is he? He has fewer friends than I do."

"It just draws attention to things we'd rather not have people know about. That's all," Felix explained, frustrated. Why couldn't Maisie admit this could be a problem?

They walked along Memorial Boulevard in silence, each lost in his and her own private thoughts.

Maisie couldn't stop thinking about the Romanov family: the Grand Duchesses and the Tsarevich all held prisoner, all murdered. Did they know what was in store for them?

After Felix calmed down about his sister, his thoughts turned to Alex Andropov and this blood disease he suffered from. Here was a kid in his grade, a kid he passed a million times in the hallway, and Felix had never once paid any attention to him or his problems. Felix knew Alex missed a lot of school. But Bitsy Beal had told him that Alex's father was a billionaire and that the family often went away on their private jet or yacht. Leave it to Bitsy Beal to get it completely wrong! The Lloyd Edward House on

Spring Street was obviously not the home of a billionaire. And Alex spent all those missed days of school in hospitals or at home in bed. Suffering, Felix remembered with a shudder.

Felix broke the silence. "I'm going to be friends with Alex," he said firmly. "He shouldn't be so alone."

"Do you think he's really a descendant of the Romanovs?" Maisie asked. "I don't. I think it's a story his grandmother or someone made up to make him feel better about his illness."

"Why do you always have to think the worst of people?" Felix said. "Maybe he is a Romanov. Maybe he would be Tsar if things had turned out differently."

Maisie laughed at the idea.

"Right. Tsar Alex of Newport."

"He wouldn't be in Newport if there hadn't been a revolution," Felix reminded her. "He'd be in Russia."

Maisie stopped walking right in front of Felix, blocking his path.

"Why do *you* always think the *best* of everyone?" she demanded.

"I don't know," Felix admitted. "But I'm glad I'm that way."

He nudged his sister aside and continued toward Bellevue Avenue and Elm Medona.

Reluctantly, scowling, Maisie followed him. When they left the Lloyd Edward House, Alex had looked so sad. *Maybe I'll come to your house sometime soon,* he'd said. Of course Felix had told him that was a great idea, and Maisie was probably going to have to be super nice to Alex for the rest of middle school.

When Maisie and Felix turned onto Bellevue Avenue, Felix paused.

"I have the weirdest feeling," he said, looking right and then left and then behind them. "Like we're being followed," he added.

"Why would anyone follow *us*?" Maisie asked.

Felix shrugged. "I thought I heard footsteps behind us, but then when I turned around, no one was there."

Maisie glanced behind them, too, just to satisfy her brother. And of course the street was empty.

The mansions there stood sentry over the street from behind tall stone walls and ornate wrought-iron gates. Compared to the Winter Palace in St. Petersburg or the Catherine Palace in Tsarskoe Selo, the Newport mansions were not so grand, Great-Uncle Thorne had told them. Maisie couldn't imagine even more enormous, fancier places than the mansions here on Bellevue Avenue. But if Great-Uncle Thorne had his way, she'd see them for herself soon enough.

A butler opened the enormous front doors of Elm Medona, and Maisie and Felix walked inside. But Felix paused in the doorway and spun around quickly, as if he would find someone standing there. But all he found were the towering elms and the low, almost eerie whistle of the wind.

"There's so much to be done!" Great-Uncle Thorne said impatiently as soon as Maisie and Felix got home.

He had been pacing in the foyer ever since three fifteen, when he had expected them to return. It was now almost six.

"Your mother's going to walk in the door any minute, and then we'll have to have dinner, creating yet another delay in opening the egg. And you two lallygaggers don't show up for three hours!" he continued.

"We've been studying Imperial Russia," Maisie told him, which was, in fact, mostly true.

Felix smiled at his sister's excuse. "Preparing," Felix added.

"You always tell us to prepare, don't you?" Maisie asked sweetly.

Great-Uncle Thorne glared at her from beneath his voluminous eyebrows.

Aiofe appeared in the foyer, looking confused. Her black-and-white maid's uniform, complete with the odd poufy bonnet she wore, seemed hastily put on, a bit lopsided and crooked.

"I thought Maisie and Felix were going to be home hours ago," Aiofe explained. "I had their snacks ready at three thirty, but now . . . well . . . the staff ate them."

"That's all right," Felix told her. "We've had a lot to eat this afternoon."

"*Blini* and *pirozhki*," Maisie said to Great-Uncle Thorne, who glared harder.

"So, I'm excused?" Aiofe asked hesitantly.

"Yes! Go!" Great-Uncle Thorne thundered.

As Aiofe scurried off, Great-Uncle Thorne raised his eyes to the ceiling and groaned, "I'm surrounded by nincompoops!"

He lowered his gaze, landing it right on Maisie and Felix.

"You two," he muttered, shaking his head, "follow me."

"Where are we going?" Felix asked nervously. After what he'd learned today about the fate of the Romanovs and revolution, this was not a trip he was eager to take.

"The Map Room!" Great-Uncle Thorne said, slapping his own forehead. "Isn't that where we've been trying to go ever since your mother barged in on us?"

Maisie and Felix followed him up the Grand Staircase. But halfway up, Great-Uncle Thorne stopped.

"Where are they?" he asked.

"Who?" Maisie said, confused.

"Why are you bumfuzzled?" Great-Uncle Thorne bellowed.

"Bumfuzzled?" Maisie repeated.

Great-Uncle Thorne raised his arms in the air and barked, "The Ziff twins! Where. Are. The. Ziff. Twins."

"Buenos Aires," Felix answered.

"Argentina? They've gone to Argentina?"

"Their father was sent there," Felix explained.

"CIA," Maisie added.

Great-Uncle Thorne's face twisted and contorted with indecision ever so briefly.

"Onward!" he finally announced.

Then he turned around and began up the stairs again, pounding his walking stick against each one as he climbed.

Maisie and Felix walked with Great-Uncle Thorne through the long corridor outside his room, Great-Aunt Maisie's, and a suite of guest rooms. They didn't usually come down this far, since Maisie had insisted they go inside every guest room months ago. Even she got bored with them eventually. Each room was spacious, with a sitting room and oversize bathroom. The beds were so high that small footstools were provided so the guests could climb up into bed. And each room had a color theme: lavender, aqua, sea-foam green, lemon yellow, eggshell. The bedspreads and pillows, the small sofas and wingback chairs, the towels, and even the soaps were all in that room's particular color. For all the whimsy and quirks of the rest of Elm Medona, the guest rooms—though fancy with gold-trimmed this and silver-accented that—were remarkably dull.

Now Great-Uncle Thorne was leading Maisie and Felix farther than they had ever ventured, past the Lavender Room, the Aqua Room, the Sea-Foam-Green Room, the Lemon-Yellow Room, the Eggshell Room. He flung open the next door, and a cloud of dust exploded from it.

Great-Uncle Thorne sneezed, waving his hands to clear the air.

"No one has been in here for quite some time," he said.

"I guess not," Maisie said.

From the doorway, the three of them stared into the Map Room.

Dust motes danced in the light that came through the row of tall windows that made up the far wall. The other three walls were murals of the continents, each country painted in bright colors, each river a vivid blue, the mountain ranges dark green and snowcapped, the oceans a shimmering turquoise.

Maisie recognized some of the countries Mrs. Witherspoon had talked about this morning in class. She saw Rhodesia and Abyssinia and the Belgian Congo on the continent of Africa.

"My goodness," Great-Uncle Thorne said in a low voice. "This room has been closed off for years, since Maisie and I studied geography and history over there."

He pointed to two wooden desks in the center of the room, facing the mural of Europe.

"My goodness," he said again, his voice even softer this time.

Great-Uncle Thorne stepped inside, almost reverentially, and walked over to the desks. Maisie and Felix watched as he traced something carved into the top of one of them, his face wistful. He dipped his finger into a hole in one corner, then held it up to examine.

"The ink," he said. "All dried up."

Slowly, he lifted the top of the desk.

Great-Uncle Thorne gasped when he peered inside it.

Maisie nudged Felix to follow her into the Map Room, but he hung back. Something about the way Great-Uncle Thorne looked made Felix feel like they should stay out here. But of course Maisie marched right over to Great-Uncle Thorne.

"Old notebooks," she said, also peering inside.

Carefully, Great-Uncle Thorne lifted a pale blue notebook from inside the desk.

Maisie saw THORNE PICKWORTH written on the cover, and beneath it WORLD HISTORY AND GEOGRAPHY.

Felix watched as Great-Uncle Thorne opened the notebook and began to read to himself, his lips moving ever so slightly.

After what seemed a long while, Great-Uncle Thorne closed the notebook and lowered the top of the desk, once again tracing something carved in the wood there.

"It seems like yesterday," he said to himself.

Maisie watched his finger as it traced the shape of a heart. Inside that carved heart were the letters *TP + PM*.

"Great-Uncle Thorne!" Maisie said. "That's you, isn't it? *TP* is Thorne Pickworth!"

Great-Uncle Thorne, maybe for the first time since Maisie had known him, blushed.

"But who's *PM*?" Maisie asked.

"Penelope Merriweather!" Felix blurted from the doorway.

"Oh!" Maisie said. "You've loved her forever!"

"Poppycock," Great-Uncle Thorne said, but he smiled as he said it.

Maisie turned her attention to the other desk. Although nothing was carved there, Great-Aunt Maisie had drawn a picture that covered the entire top of her desk. The colors were so faded that it was difficult to make out the images. But slowly, as Maisie stared at it, they began to take shape. A wooden roller coaster. A Ferris wheel. A boardwalk. Blurry figures on what appeared to be a beach with a wave washing up against it.

"Coney Island!" Maisie exclaimed.

Great-Uncle Thorne sighed.

"Yes," he said begrudgingly, "that's Maisie's drawing of Coney Island. I'm glad to see the thing fading away."

"That's where she met Harry Houdini," Felix said.

"The beginning of the end," Great-Uncle Thorne said with another sigh.

Finally Felix walked into the room, too. Almost immediately he caught sight of an enormous globe in the corner. The globe stood taller than him, taller than Great-Uncle Thorne, and so wide that Felix wouldn't be able to fit his arms around it. What really struck him, though, even more than the sheer size of the thing, was how part of it was in shadow and part was in light.

Felix blinked.

"Hey!" he said. "This globe . . . It's . . . spinning!"

Great-Uncle Thorne let out a whoop.

"Still? After all these years?" Great-Uncle Thorne said with delight.

He went and stood beside Felix to watch the globe turn almost imperceptibly on its axis.

"Is it rotating like we are?" Maisie asked as she joined them in front of the globe.

"Exactly," Great-Uncle Thorne said, nodding.

He walked right up to the globe and picked up a long wooden pointer like Mrs. Witherspoon used, except even longer.

"So it's six thirty here in Newport, Rhode Island," Great-Uncle Thorne said, pointing to the speck on the east coast of the United States, "and we've still got some light. But over here in . . . Let's see . . ."

He walked around to the other side of the globe and grinned, pointing the pointer.

"In Paris it's after midnight and therefore, completely dark."

"How is it doing that?" Felix asked.

"Only Phinneas Pickworth himself could explain that, I'm afraid," Great-Uncle Thorne said. "He brought this home from Florence, Italy, on one of his expeditions. I can't believe the old thing is as good as new."

Out of the corner of her eye, Maisie caught sight of Imperial Russia stretching across the wall nearest her.

"Well," she said, turning toward it, "I suppose it's time for you to tell us about this."

Great-Uncle Thorne squinted at what she was studying.

"Ah," he said, "yes, indeed. Imperial Russia. The Tsar Nicholas and Tsarina Alexandra. It's best you two are prepared before we open that egg and find out what exactly you have to do."

Maisie's head was spinning with Russian history, hard-to-pronounce and harder-to-remember names, and all the other details and facts that Great-Uncle Thorne was giving them. The room had grown dark, and Great-Uncle Thorne had turned on lamps that gave a golden glow to everything. She wondered where her mother was. Her stomach growled with hunger. Would Great-Uncle Thorne ever stop talking?

"You could end up here," Great-Uncle Thorne was saying. "Every March the royal family left the cold and snow of St. Petersburg for the warmth of Crimea, on the northern coast of the Black Sea."

Felix's eyes shone with excitement as he watched Great-Uncle Thorne's long wooden pointer land in Crimea on the mural.

"Of course," Great-Uncle Thorne mused, the pointer hovering in the air, "you could land on the Imperial train, en route to Crimea. Approximately a two- or three-day trip. Or you could land here in the villa on the Baltic . . ."

The pointer landed again with a sharp rap, causing Maisie to jump.

"Villa," she said when Great-Uncle Thorne frowned at her with disapproval. "Baltic."

He turned back to Imperial Russia.

"I'm hungry," Maisie moaned.

"The *Standart*," Great-Uncle Thorne said, more to himself than to Maisie and Felix. "They could land on the *Standart*."

Maisie followed the pointer as it moved up to Finland and traced a curving path along the fjords there.

"Is the *Standart* a boat?" Felix asked.

Isn't he hungry? Maisie wondered as her stomach growled again.

"Ha!" Great-Uncle Thorne said, facing them again with his cheeks flushed red. "Hardly! The *Standart* is the Imperial yacht, and every June the royal family cruised the Finnish coast on it."

"Royal yacht. Royal train—"

"*Imperial* train," Great-Uncle Thorne corrected.

"Same thing," Maisie said miserably. "We get it. They moved around all year on their royal stuff, from villa to castle."

"It might save your life to know these things," Great-Uncle Thorne said sternly.

He held Maisie's gaze until she rolled her eyes and looked away.

Great-Uncle Thorne still stared at her for a long moment before he began pointing at other places on the mural.

"August would find you in the lodge in the Polish forest. September, back to Crimea. Winter . . ."

He stopped speaking and pointing.

Silence filled the room.

"Are we done?" Maisie finally asked hopefully.

"Winter," Great-Uncle Thorne said again.

He slowly turned to face them.

"Winter in St. Petersburg," Great-Uncle Thorne said. "From November till March, the city remains extremely chilly, with temperatures no higher than minus ten Celsius. With no more than twenty hours of sunshine per month."

Maisie converted Celsius to Fahrenheit in her head. Fourteen degrees. That was cold. She shivered.

"In other words, I can't send you without the proper clothing. Even if you land in beautiful Crimea or on the *Standart*, it's entirely possible you'll stay through several seasons—"

"But we'll leave before July 1917," Felix added quickly.

"Of course," Great-Uncle Thorne said. "Of course."

And unconvincingly, Felix thought.

Great-Uncle Thorne cleared his throat.

"The point is, you need to have the proper clothing, or you could freeze to death," Great-Uncle Thorne said.

"This doesn't make sense," Maisie said, narrowing her eyes at her uncle. "You've never ever told us where to go, or helped us get there, or anything."

"He's only looking out for us," Felix told her. "I think it's nice."

"But every other time, we landed in whatever we had on and made do—" Maisie began to protest.

"This time," Great-Uncle Thorne boomed, banging his fist down hard on one of the desks, "you can't just *make do*. This time, you must be prepared. For anything."

"Why?" Maisie asked.

"Because this time is different," Great-Uncle Thorne said, sinking onto the chair that was attached to the wooden desk. "This time you will be taking the lost Fabergé egg with you. This time something is going to happen. Something wonderful."

Great-Uncle Thorne's eyes took on the yellow light of the lamps.

He sighed. "I wish I knew what it was. But I don't. I only know that the lost egg has been found. That Amy Pickworth has spoken to us across time and space. That *something* special, something unforgettable, is going to occur in Imperial Russia."

Great-Uncle Thorne sighed again.

"It's too complicated for me to explain," he said, shaking his head. "Why, sometimes I'm not sure I completely understand it myself. But Phinneas called our ability to time travel and for events to happen simultaneously in different times and places the Pickworth Paradoxia Perpetuity."

"The Pickworth Paradoxia Perpetuity," Felix said in a hushed voice.

"Yes," Great-Uncle Thorne said solemnly. "It's so complex, so amazing, so . . . mind-boggling, that even I can barely understand it myself."

Maisie and Felix's mother's voice cut through the heavy silence that descended after Great-Uncle Thorne's words.

"Another secret room?" she said, coming inside.

Right behind her came Bruce Fishbaum, looking more nautical than ever in his Nantucket-red pants and navy blue belt with little white whales, and a white shirt with some yacht club logo on it.

"This house is huge!" Bruce Fishbaum exclaimed. His face was pink, his hairline receding even more.

"Indeed," Great-Uncle Thorne said, his voice dripping with displeasure.

"So this room is . . . ?" their mother asked, glancing around.

"The Map Room," Felix answered, since no one else was going to. "Great-Uncle Thorne and Great-Aunt Maisie used to learn history and geography here."

"Really?" his mother cooed. "That's amazing. Isn't that amazing?" she asked Bruce Fishbaum.

He laughed his guffawing laugh. "Amazing!"

"We were just talking about Peter Carl Fabergé," Great-Uncle Thorne said.

"We were?" Maisie asked.

But Great-Uncle Thorne ignored her. "You've heard of him?"

"Sure," Bruce Fishbaum said. "He made the fancy eggs."

"Yes," Great-Uncle Thorne said, "he did. Fabergé was the official court jeweler to the Tsar of Russia."

"You don't say," Bruce Fishbaum said in a way that made it hard for Maisie to know if he was really interested or not.

"At the turn of the last century, he employed over five hundred people in his St. Petersburg workshop. Of course, he designed more than the eggs. Little cases and jewelry and his miniatures of flowers and animals and the like. My mother actually had a diamond-encrusted miniature Pickworth peony designed by Fabergé."

"Is that so?" Bruce Fishbaum said in that same tone.

"But it's the eggs that everyone remembers. The first one was made for Tsarina Marie as a gift from her husband, Tsar Alexander, in 1885. The brilliance of the eggs, of course, is that the egg is just a container for the surprise inside. For example, the peacock egg of 1908. The surprise is a mechanical gold and enameled peacock, sitting in the branches of an engraved gold tree with flowers made of enamel and precious stones. The peacock can be lifted from within the tree and wound up. Placed on a flat surface, it struts around, moving its head and spreads and closes its enamel tail."

"You don't say," Bruce Fishbaum said.

Great-Uncle Thorne's face lit with excitement. "Or the rock crystal egg. Inside the rock crystal egg is a gold support holding twelve miniature paintings of the various palaces and residences significant to the empress Alexandra. Each location holds a special memory for Nicholas and Alexandra in the early days of their courtship. They were newlyweds when the Tsar gave it to her in 1896, after all.

"The large emerald on the apex can be depressed to engage a mechanism that rotates the miniatures inside the egg. Then a hook moves down and folds the framed pictures back, like the pages of a book, so two paintings can be fully seen at one time. Each miniature is framed in gold with an emerald on its apex."

He clapped his hands together in delight.

"But the pièce de résistance—" Great-Uncle Thorne began.

"You certainly know your Fabergé eggs," Maisie and Felix's mother said kindly. "But I came up searching for these two so Bruce and I could take them to his house for dinner."

"My kids are home from boarding school, so I thought, Hey! Let's get them all together," Bruce said.

"He bought steaks to grill," their mother said.

"Most people believe Fabergé made fifty-eight eggs," Great-Uncle Thorne continued, despite the looks their mother and Bruce shot each other.

"Only fifty-eight," Bruce said. "How about that."

"I said, *most* people believe there were fifty-eight," Great-Uncle Thorne corrected.

"Right-o," Bruce said, shrugging.

"But they would be wrong, those people," Great-Uncle Thorne said, getting to his feet.

"O-kay," Bruce said slowly.

"Bruce got that macaroni salad you like, Maisie," her mother said. "The one from the Sunshine Deli."

Great-Uncle Thorne was struggling with the clasps on the valise he'd brought with him into the Map Room.

"Let me give you a hand, there," Bruce said, bending to help.

But Great-Uncle Thorne shooed him away.

Finally, the clasps popped open and Great-Uncle Thorne reached inside, removing something wrapped in pale pink tissue paper.

He set the object on the desk, then carefully unwrapped the tissue from it.

Their mother gasped.

"Whoa," Bruce Fishbaum said softly.

"Here it is," Great-Uncle Thorne said, his liver-spotted hand resting on the very tip of the lost egg. "The fifty-ninth Fabergé egg."

CHAPTER FOUR

THE SURPRISE

"Wh . . . where did you get *that*?" Maisie and Felix's mother stammered.

Great-Uncle Thorne placed the egg on his old desk so that everyone could get a good look at it.

Larger than a baseball, beneath all of its ornamentation the egg was the purest white. Whiter than fresh snow. Whiter than clouds or angel hair. Four ribbons of gold radiated from its top, along the delicate curve of the egg, and all the way to the bottom. Each ribbon had a different motif carved into it. Cherubs. Roses. Wolves' heads. And what appeared to be interlocking letter *R*s.

Then there were the jewels. Sapphires and diamonds bigger than marbles formed a cap at the top and covered the bottom. They sparkled as if they had just been polished, revealing every shade of blue imaginable. Cobalt and navy and midnight and sky. The diamonds, too, were different shades. Champagne and pink and yellow and eggshell.

They all stood—Great-Uncle Thorne, Maisie, Felix, their mother, and Bruce Fishbaum—leaning forward, marveling at the egg, at how many diamonds and sapphires covered it. All of them a slightly different color, all of them so smooth.

Bruce Fishbaum frowned.

"There's a flaw," he announced.

"Doubtful," Great-Uncle Thorne said.

"All these diamonds and sapphires are perfect and shiny," Bruce said. "Except one."

Maisie and Felix looked at each other and then back at the egg.

Bruce Fishbaum's hand paused over a particularly deep blue sapphire. So dark, in fact, that it almost looked black.

"This one," he said. "It doesn't shine like the others. In fact, it's dull. And rougher cut."

Great-Uncle Thorne smiled that smile he gave Maisie and Felix when he was indulging their stupidity.

"What did I tell you about Fabergé eggs?" he asked, not even trying to mask his condescension.

Bruce shrugged. "They were made for the Tsars? Of Russia?"

"Obviously," Great-Uncle Thorne said.

"They have surprises inside," Maisie and Felix's mother said.

"Exactly, Jennifer," Great-Uncle Thorne said. "And one must be able to get inside to find the surprise."

"Ah!" Bruce Fishbaum said, nodding. "So that's the way in. Open it up and let's see if there's a cuckoo or something inside."

"Unfortunately," Great-Uncle Thorne said, "the mechanism on this particular egg is broken."

Maisie and Felix both looked up, surprised.

"So the surprise will remain a mystery, I'm afraid."

"But—" Maisie began.

Great-Uncle Thorne shot her a look as sharp as daggers.

"What a shame," Bruce Fishbaum said.

He glanced down at his watch.

"Hate to break up this little party," he said, "but

I've got two hungry kids at home waiting for a steak dinner."

"Uncle Thorne," Maisie and Felix's mother said, "this egg should go into a vault or something. Or a museum."

Great-Uncle Thorne nodded. "You're absolutely right," he said. "It needs to find a proper home."

"You mean that's the object?" Maisie blurted.

Immediately she clamped her hand over her mouth.

"What object?" her mother asked.

"Um . . . ," Felix said. "The fifty-ninth Fabergé egg."

"Well, isn't that what Uncle Thorne said?" his mother said.

"Yes. Yes it is," Felix agreed.

Maisie nodded too enthusiastically.

"Are you two up to something?" their mother asked, narrowing her eyes at them as if to see them better.

"No," Maisie said, as innocently as she could manage.

Felix just smiled at their mother.

"Let's get going," Bruce Fishbaum said.

He touched Great-Uncle Thorne's arm as he

made his way out of the Map Room.

"If you need some advice about where to put that egg, give me a call," he said.

❄

All Maisie wanted to do was open that egg.

Instead, she and Felix were trapped for hours at Bruce Fishbaum's house with his kids, both of them decked out in athletic wear from head to toe: the boy, Todd, in shiny black pants with their boarding-school name climbing one leg in bloodred, a shirt announcing he was on the school hockey team, and a Patriots' baseball hat; the girl, Cate, in a short lacrosse kilt, a polo shirt with the school name on it with crossed sticks beneath it, and a pink visor with the logo of a yacht club.

Bruce Fishbaum grilled steaks while Maisie and Felix's mother made a salad, and the four kids stood awkwardly in the backyard, trying to think of things to say to one another.

Cate tried. "I really don't like lacrosse," she said, flipping her pale blond hair back. "Ice hockey's my game."

"We're an ice-hockey family," Todd said smugly.

"Then why do you play lacrosse if you don't like

it?" Felix asked her politely.

Cate looked at him, confused. "You need a spring sport," she said.

Todd nodded in agreement. He was tall, well over six feet, and burly, with blond hair several shades darker than his sister's and thick wide hands. His nose, Maisie thought, reminded her of a ski jump. Cate had a similar one, but smaller.

Felix tried: "Maisie got the lead in the school play!"

Cate and Todd stared back at him blankly.

Maisie wondered if those steaks would ever get cooked so they could eat and go home and finally open the egg.

"*The Crucible,*" Felix added.

"We do this Follies show at school," Todd said. "And all the hockey players dress like girls."

"It's hilarious," Cate said.

They all shifted on their feet for a bit.

Then Todd tried: "You guys moved here from New York, right?"

"Yes," Felix said, happy to find something to talk about. "We lived in Greenwich Village, on Bethune Street."

"My roommate lives on East Seventy-Seventh Street," Todd said. "Matt Homes. You know him?"

"No," Felix said.

Thankfully, Bruce Fishbaum called everyone to dinner. He and Maisie and Felix's mother had a short discussion on whether or not it was too cold to eat outside, and finally they decided it was. So they all picked up a plate and a napkin and silverware from the teak table outside and rearranged themselves in a room that the Fishbaums called the sunroom. It reminded Maisie of a greenhouse, with glass slanted walls, a glass roof, a big ficus tree in one corner, and a tree with small oranges in another. The sunroom was hot as a greenhouse, too, and Maisie could smell Todd Fishbaum's locker-room scent and Cate Fishbaum's fruity shampoo.

The steaks were enormous and bloody. Felix didn't like bloody meat, and he grew pale just looking at the slab of beef on his plate. Unlike Maisie, Felix was in no hurry to get home and open the egg. Because once they did, they would have to go to Imperial Russia, where for all he knew the Bolsheviks were wreaking havoc and murdering people. He didn't really like the awkwardness here at the

Fishbaums', and Cate and Todd seemed like creatures from another planet to Felix. But at least it was safe here. No Bolsheviks lurked around corners. No one was trying to massacre anyone else.

"Bruce," Felix's mother was saying, her hand on Bruce's thick forearm, "do you think you could throw Felix's steak on the grill for a few more minutes? He doesn't like it rare."

The Fishbaums turned their heads toward Felix in unison, their faces shocked.

"You lose the nutrients that way," Bruce said to Felix. "The iron and whatnot."

Felix looked down at the steak, which by now was sitting in a small bloody puddle.

"It's your call, buddy," Bruce Fishbaum said, swiping up Felix's plate and heading out of the sunroom.

"Thank you," Felix called after him, but Bruce was already lifting the hood of the grill and tossing the steak inside, shaking his head as he did.

Todd and Cate chewed their steak, their eyes fixed on Felix. There was nothing else to eat, except the macaroni salad. But the blood from the steak had oozed across the plate, so Felix just sat, watching the Fishbaum kids chew.

※

"Wasn't that fun?" Maisie and Felix's mother asked them as they drove, finally, back to Elm Medona.

"Really fun," Felix said, to be nice.

"Todd Fishbaum is an oaf," Maisie said, jiggling her leg as if that would help them get home faster.

"Maisie!" her mother reprimanded. "He's a star ice-hockey player, you know. And a very nice boy."

Usually, Maisie would argue her point. But tonight she chose to focus instead on what was inside that egg. Great-Uncle Thorne's description of the other eggs and the surprises they held had captivated her imagination. But this egg was even more special, wasn't it? And Amy Pickworth had spoken to them across time and ordered them to open it. *Why?* Maisie wondered. *Why now?*

At last Elm Medona came into view.

The tall black wrought-iron gates trimmed in gold leaf with the interlocking *P*s in the center slowly swung open, and they made their way up the long winding road that led to Elm Medona.

Maisie expected to find Great-Uncle Thorne

anxiously waiting in the foyer. But inside the mansion was empty, the lights turned low.

"Great-Uncle Thorne?" Maisie called out.

"Shhh," her mother hushed. "Let the poor man rest. He was at death's door days ago. He needs to sleep and recover."

Maisie looked at Felix, who was acting like he was about to go up to bed himself.

"Well, that was a great steak," he said to his mother.

He yawned and headed for the Grand Staircase.

"I'm going to read a little and then go to sleep," he added over his shoulder.

Maisie stomped off after him.

"Good night, Maisie," her mother said in that tone that meant Maisie had misbehaved.

"Good night," Maisie muttered, hurrying to catch up with Felix.

As she passed the photograph of Great-Aunt Maisie as a girl Maisie's own age, she paused. Sometimes it seemed like Great-Aunt Maisie was smiling at her from that picture. Like now.

"What do you know?" Maisie whispered, and waited as if the girl in the picture might actually answer her.

Of course that didn't happen, and Maisie continued on her way upstairs.

Instead of going to the Princess Annabelle of Nanuh's Room, though, she went straight to Samuel Dormatorio, where Felix was already in his pajamas, a book in his hand.

"What are you doing?" Maisie asked him in frustration. "We have to open the egg!"

"I figured if Great-Uncle Thorne wanted us to do it now, he would have been waiting for us. I guess it's not as urgent as we thought?"

Maisie studied her brother's face carefully.

"You're scared," she said finally.

"Scared? Me?" Felix asked. "Of Bolsheviks and massacres? Not at all."

"We'll be long gone before the Bolsheviks arrive," Maisie said.

Felix pointed a finger at her. "You don't know that."

"I don't *know* know it," Maisie said.

"Exactly," Felix said, and he climbed into his big bed, the bull's head staring down at him.

Maisie tried a different tactic.

"Do you really think Great-Uncle Thorne would

put us in danger?" she asked.

Felix lowered the book he'd stuck his face in.

"Yes," he answered and lifted the book again.

Maisie tried to think of what else she could say to persuade her brother to go right now with her, find Great-Uncle Thorne, and open the egg.

Felix kept reading, turning the page every now and then as if she wasn't even standing there.

Finally, exasperated, Maisie gave up.

She left Samuel Dormatorio, being sure to pound her feet hard enough to make her point.

Back in her own room, Maisie paced, trying to come up with a plan. But after a lot of pacing and thinking, she had not one single good idea.

Why did Felix have to be so impossible sometimes?

Maisie wished she could call Hadley Ziff and complain to her. Hadley would understand; Rayne drove her crazy in exactly the same way. But it was impossible to call someone in Buenos Aires, especially without any information on exactly where that someone was.

Outside the two big windows, the moon was a

perfect sliver in the inky sky. Maisie wandered over to one of the windows and gazed out. She couldn't remember seeing quite this many stars before. Or such bright ones. They twinkled down at her as if they were lighting a path upward.

When she was little, her mother always reminded her to make a wish on a star.

Maisie chose one that seemed to be the twinkliest.

Star light, star bright, she thought. *First star I see tonight, I wish I may, I wish I might have the wish I wish tonight.*

Out loud she said, "I wish Felix changes his mind and comes in here and helps me find Great-Uncle Thorne and open the egg tonight."

She frowned.

Would that count as four wishes?

No, she decided. All those things together equaled her one wish.

She squeezed her eyes shut, willing it to come true.

A small explosion sounded from somewhere in the vicinity of her closet, followed by Great-Uncle Thorne booming: "It's about time you rapscallions got home from that Fishbag's house!"

Startled and delighted at the same time, Maisie turned from the window just in time to see Great-Uncle Thorne emerge from . . . yes . . . her closet. In his arms he had a large pile of clothes. Dead animals appeared to be draped over his shoulder.

"Fish*baum*," Maisie giggled.

"Did you devour a big bloody American steak?" Great-Uncle Thorne said with disgust.

Maisie giggled some more. "I did," she admitted.

"Disgusting," Great-Uncle Thorne said as he dropped the clothes and dead animals on the bed.

"But what can one expect from a grown man wearing a belt with tiny whales on it?" Great-Uncle Thorne continued, more to himself, it seemed, than to Maisie.

Still, Maisie agreed. "Ridiculous," she said.

The dead animals, she realized, were not, in fact, dead animals but the fur of animals. Piles of white fur and piles of brown fur.

"Have you been skinning animals in my closet?" she asked Great-Uncle Thorne.

"I've been preparing items for your imminent departure," he said.

With that he disappeared back into the closet.

Maisie heard him grunt, then the sounds of something being dragged across the floor in there.

Great-Uncle Thorne came back out, walking backward and bent.

"What's *that*?" Maisie asked.

Great-Uncle Thorne didn't need to answer.

By the time the question was asked, he had fully exited the closet, and Maisie saw that he had dragged out with him a large black trunk with gold corners.

She frowned at it, confused.

This was, after all, *her* closet. And Maisie knew for certain that there was no large black trunk with gold corners in there.

There used to be the small chest of old clothes, the one where she'd found the costume for Bitsy Beal's March Madness party. Maisie shuddered remembering that terrible night. It had been so terrible that she'd thrown the clothes back inside and put the chest itself in one of the guest-room closets so she'd never have to see it again.

Great-Uncle Thorne had opened this trunk with the gold corners and was busily digging through it. From time to time he lifted up a garment for inspection and either tossed it on top of the furs or back into the trunk. As he did this, he whistled softly, a tune Maisie didn't recognize. He completely ignored her, so Maisie took a look in her closet.

To her surprise, what she had always assumed was the back wall had disappeared. The closet stretched back into a second, smaller room. Maisie's clothes had been pushed aside for easier access into the room, and she went in there now.

The room was indeed small, but large enough for a coatrack, from which all kinds of coats hung: velvet, lace, embroidered. A hat rack held hats with feathers and veils and bunches of fruit and jewels. Maisie could see the rectangle where the trunk had been, that part of the floor a lighter shade than the rest. On the walls hung travel posters from Trans World Airlines, bright illustrations of exotic places with drawings of airplanes on them. In one corner, on a narrow desk, stood stacks of old postcards. Maisie picked one up and saw the faded signature: YOURS, MAISIE PICKWORTH.

"I think we're ready!" Great-Uncle Thorne called from the closet door.

Maisie took one more look around this strange room before she made her way back out.

"What is that place?" she asked.

"Why, the Voyage Room, of course," Great-Uncle Thorne said without looking up at her. He pronounced *voyage* like *voy-ah-ge*.

"The Voyage Room," Maisie repeated, imitating Great-Uncle Thorne's pronunciation.

"I believe we are ready," he said.

From his breast pocket he pulled out an envelope.

"I just need to add the Pickworth seal to this, and then we shall open the egg and . . ."

Great-Uncle Thorne paused.

"Where's your brother?" he asked, as if he'd just noticed Felix was absent.

"In bed," Maisie said.

"Bed?" Great-Uncle Thorne bellowed. "On this most important night?"

Maisie nodded.

"Well, go and get him out of bed!" he ordered her.

"She doesn't have to," Felix said in a tremulous voice from the doorway. "I'm here."

What Felix realized as he lay in bed avoiding this very moment, was that if he did do Great-Uncle Thorne's bidding this one last time, it might indeed be the very last time. And then he could go back to his normal life as a kid at Anne Hutchinson Elementary School. If it was time to open the egg, then he would do it. He would see what was inside, and then he would do whatever was required of him, because this might put an end to The Treasure Chest. No more getting chased, locked up, thrown overboard, fleeing, hiding, running, or losing Maisie.

No more adventures.

No more time travel.

The thought made Felix smile.

So he got up and made his way to the Princess Room, where Maisie and Great-Uncle Thorne were preparing to open the egg.

He had to admit that he was surprised to find no egg in sight. Instead, there were clothes and furs everywhere.

"Good!" Great-Uncle Thorne exclaimed, his eyes shining.

He looked through the pile of clothes and began pulling out items and tossing them in Felix's direction. Almost simultaneously he tossed other items at Maisie, who scooped them up with great delight.

"You need to be prepared," Great-Uncle Thorne muttered.

Maisie held an embroidered white silk dress up to her and skipped over to the full-length mirror.

"No, no!" Great-Uncle Thorne called to her. "There are three pieces to that."

He showed her a velvet dress and another white silk piece with more embroidery.

"And, of course, there's the *tiare Russe*," he added, lifting a jewel-studded crown up for Maisie to see.

"I get to wear that?" she exclaimed, racing back to Great-Uncle Thorne.

She took the tiara from him and placed it on her head, surprised by how heavy it was.

"My neck's going to break!" she complained.

"You won't wear it all the time," Great-Uncle Thorne said, plucking it from her head and placing it along with the three-piece dress into the trunk.

Maisie watched as he added a long white fur coat with a matching hat and muff to the trunk.

"Now, Felix," Great-Uncle Thorne said. "Put this on."

"I'm not wearing this!" Felix said, studying what Great-Uncle Thorne had thrown his way.

Maisie laughed. "That's funny," she said.

That was a white blousy shirt with a large navy blue sailor collar that fell behind the back.

"And yours," Great-Uncle Thorne was saying, ignoring both their delight and their complaints. "You have to put this on, too, Maisie."

He handed Maisie a very similar piece of clothing, except hers was a drop-waist dress.

"Ugh!" she said. "Why do we have to dress like sailors?"

Great-Uncle Thorne didn't answer. He was too busy adding items to the trunk: a military-looking coat and breeches for Felix; a white lace dress and pearls for Maisie; a black fur coat and hat for Felix. He didn't pay any attention to either of them until the trunk was full. Then he sighed and stepped back to admire his choices before closing the gold latch.

"Go! Change your clothes!" he shouted, escorting them to the door so they could go and change.

Reluctantly, they obeyed, returning to the room in their ridiculous sailor suits, feeling awkward and silly. They both had their shards around their necks, too.

Great-Uncle Thorne surveyed them. He nodded approvingly.

"Now," he said, "you two will arrive suitably dressed. And you'll be prepared for anything. A ball. Ice skating. Formal dinners. Anything."

Maisie took a deep breath.

"Is it time?" she asked hopefully.

Great-Uncle Thorne got a faraway look in his eyes.

"How I wish I could go with you," he said wistfully. "What wonders await you!"

Felix swallowed hard, trying to calm himself. What if they didn't come back? What if he never saw his mother or father again? He thought of his mother's bacon-and-egg pasta, of her cool hand on his forehead when he got sick. He thought of his father's hearty laugh, the way he smelled like paint and turpentine and the spicy cologne he sometimes wore.

"Are you *crying*?" Maisie asked him.

Felix shook his head, willing the tears he felt burning his eyes not to fall.

"The final thing," Great-Uncle Thorne said, as if he had just remembered something.

Would they ever get to Russia? Maisie wondered as Great-Uncle Thorne fumbled inside his jacket pocket.

He produced an envelope of old-fashioned heavy cream paper. From the envelope he pulled a single sheet of paper.

"A letter of introduction," he explained. "Very common at the time. You show up with one of these, and there are no questions asked. It's almost like a reference letter."

"What does it say?" Maisie asked.

"It says that you are Maisie and Felix Robbins, of New York City and Newport, and that you are the relatives of Phinneas Pickworth. In fact," Great-Uncle Thorne said, a small smile tugging at the corners of his mouth, "it's signed by Phinneas himself."

"How?" Felix blurted.

"Forgery, my dear lad," Great-Uncle Thorne answered.

His hand went back inside his jacket pocket, and this time he retrieved sealing wax, a gold embossed seal, and matches.

"I shall give it the Pickworth seal," he explained, carefully folding the letter back into the envelope and placing the envelope on the top of the table beside the bed, "and then you shall be ready to go."

Felix's heart galloped.

Great-Uncle Thorne struck the match, and the smell of sulfur filled the room as the blue flame jumped to life. He carefully dripped red wax onto the envelope, then pressed the Pickworth seal into the hot wax.

"Now," he said, "the egg."

With a deep breath, Great-Uncle Thorne blew out the flame, sending them all into darkness.

"Hey!" Felix said when he realized that the lights weren't working.

"Hmm," Great-Uncle Thorne said. "It appears the electricity has gone out."

"But why?" Felix asked, his throat suddenly dry with fear. "There's not a storm or anything."

Again the sound of a match striking and the smell of sulfur filled the room. A moment later Great-Uncle Thorne's face appeared, ghostly behind two candles he'd lit.

"Peculiar," he said softly.

Maisie and Felix watched him disappear into the closet again.

This time when he came out, he had the egg with him.

"At last," he whispered, his gnarled hands caressing the jewels.

Until he reached the dark, dull sapphire.

His long finger with its yellowed fingernail paused there for a moment before pressing the sapphire.

A sound like a sigh came from it, and Felix felt the hairs stand up along his arms.

A brief hesitation, and then a small door swung open.

Great-Uncle Thorne felt around the gold edges of the door until another small sigh came from the egg. Like the wings of a butterfly, small lines of gold appeared, and each could be lifted and opened to reveal the inside of the egg.

Maisie and Felix held their breaths.

The inside of the egg was awash in lapis lazuli, the bluest of all semiprecious stones.

"Lapis lazuli," Great-Uncle Thorne said in wonder, "prized since antiquity for its color. It was used for the eyebrows in King Tutankhamen's funeral mask."

When Great-Uncle Thorne ran his finger over the smooth stone, another sigh sounded, and from the center popped a peacock. This peacock had a tail made of glittering jewels that opened and closed as it strutted across the lapis. Maisie and Felix watched, mesmerized by the gold bird with the bejeweled tail, until it stopped, opened its small ruby beak, and let out a sound like a baby crying.

"What a noise!" Maisie said, covering her ears.

But as soon as the sound stopped, the walls of the lapis swiveled to reveal mirrors that reflected the peacock hundreds of times.

The peacock once again disappeared into the floor.

The mirrors swiveled again to reveal walls covered with miniature art and icons, all of it made with sparkling jewels, gold, and silver.

Six sections of the wall opened, and from each of them a small figure emerged.

Four girls and one boy.

They were all dressed similarly, in white sailor suits.

"It's them," Felix whispered.

"Who?" Maisie whispered back.

"The Grand Duchesses and the Tsarevich," Felix said.

One of the Grand Duchesses had her hand outstretched.

In it was an alabaster envelope with a ruby for its seal.

Great-Uncle Thorne took it from her. When he touched the ruby, the top of the envelope sprang open.

"A note," Great-Uncle Thorne said.

He carefully took the alabaster letter inside it and held it out for Maisie and Felix to see.

In blue as blue as the lapis lazuli, were the words:

HELP ME

CHAPTER FIVE

THE IMPERIAL PALACE AT LIVADIA

"I'm not going," Felix said, goose bumps shooting up his back.

At the same time, Maisie said, "Let's go!"

Great-Uncle Thorne put the note back in its little envelope and the envelope back in the Grand Duchess's hand.

As soon as he did, everything happened in reverse:

The five Romanovs went behind the walls.

The walls swiveled and became mirrors.

The mirrors reflected hundreds of peacocks as the bejeweled gold one appeared, crying its cry.

The mirrors swiveled and became lapis lazuli walls.

The peacock strutted, opening and closing its tail.

The peacock disappeared beneath the lapis floor.

The butterfly-wing doors swung shut, their gold borders fading into the egg.

The dark, dull sapphire swung back into its place.

A small sigh sounded.

The three of them stared at the egg. Then at one other. Then back at the egg.

"You will put one hand here," Great-Uncle Thorne told Maisie, placing the handle of the trunk in her hand.

"And one hand here," he continued, placing her other hand on the egg.

"And *you*," he said to Felix—

But Felix stepped back, away from Great-Uncle Thorne and Maisie.

"No," he said. "I can't."

"You must," Great-Uncle Thorne said sternly.

Felix shook his head.

Or at least he tried to. His whole body was trembling so much that he couldn't tell if he had shaken his head enough to say *no* again.

"Felix," Maisie said.

"That note said, *Help me*," Felix reminded his sister.

"All the more reason to go," Great-Uncle Thorne told him.

"All the more reason to stay in my nice, safe bed," Felix countered.

"Poppycock!" Great-Uncle Thorne said.

And with that he grabbed Felix, hard, by the hand, placed Felix's hand on the egg, and just like that, they began to tumble.

Felix looked up into a bright blue sky, against which white minarets rose.

Minarets, Felix knew, were on mosques.

And mosques were Muslim.

And, he thought unhappily, Imperial Russia was Russian Orthodox, *not* Muslim.

So he hadn't landed in Russia at all, he realized with growing fear. He'd landed maybe in the Middle East, a place whose history he knew nothing about.

Felix sat up.

Before him lay a little village of whitewashed houses perched on a slope. All the information Alex Andropov and Great-Uncle Thorne had given him on Russia had not included anything like this.

The sound of pounding hooves thundered behind him, and Felix turned to see an army of men in white pants and embroidered jackets with what looked like black bushes on their heads. Bearded and dark, the men passed on their horses without any notice of Felix.

But a female voice said, "Boy? What are you doing?"

Felix saw a pair of dark eyes peering at him over a black veil that covered most of a girl's face. Her hair was bright red, and her gauzy clothes a color blue that made Felix think of that lapis lazuli.

"I think I'm lost," he said.

"You aren't Tartar," she said, matter-of-factly.

Tartar? Felix thought. No one had mentioned that. He wondered who the Tartars were and why he'd landed with them instead of with the Tsar.

"No," Felix said. "I'm not."

One thing Felix had to admit, it smelled really good here. Like flowers and fruit trees. In fact, the slopes were awash in purples—lilacs and wisteria and other plants he couldn't recognize. The girl in front of him had a basket filled with plump red strawberries. As she studied his face, she ate one, and then another.

Felix took a deep breath.

Beneath the smell of flowers, he could smell the salty air near the ocean.

"Where am I, anyway?" he asked.

"Between Yalta and Sevastopol," she said.

Felix sighed. Neither of those places sounded familiar. How would he ever find Maisie now?

"How did you get here?" the girl asked, cocking her head with curiosity.

Felix remembered Alex Andropov bragging about the Trans-Siberian railroad. *Russia built their railroad faster than any country in Europe,* he'd boasted.

Felix grinned. "Train," he offered.

The girl frowned. "The Tsar forbade the railroad from coming here," she said.

"He did?" Felix asked. *What does Alex Andropov know, anyway?* he thought.

"Except for the one track from Simferopol," she added.

Felix grinned again. "Yes, that's the one I rode on."

"And to get here from the train in Sevastopol, you took . . . ?"

She waited.

Felix took a deep breath, stalling. His nose filled with the smell of sea air.

"A boat," he said. "I took a boat."

She considered this.

"That must have taken hours," she finally concluded.

"Yes," Felix agreed. "Hours."

"And you traveled this far because . . . ?"

Felix tried to think of an answer.

"The Tsar," he said, vaguely.

"For the opening of the palace at Livadia?" she said, surprised.

"Yes!" Felix said gratefully.

Livadia. Great-Uncle Thorne had told Felix and Maisie all about it.

Relief swept over Felix. He was in Crimea.

❈

Maisie saw white. Blinding, beautiful, endless white.

She squinted against the brightness to try to better see what she was looking at.

A palace, she realized. A palace that reminded her of the palazzos she had seen in Florence, Italy, when she and Felix had met Leonardo da Vinci. For a moment, Maisie worried that things had gone terribly wrong and she'd somehow ended up with this steamer trunk and Fabergé egg in Florence.

The egg.

Maisie held it awkwardly in her hand. *This won't do at all*, she thought.

She opened the trunk, and for an instant it seemed that the things inside shifted. Maisie blinked.

No, of course they hadn't moved. She scolded herself for her overactive imagination.

She focused her attention back on the trunk and found a piece of delicate white lace inside. Unsure what its real purpose was, Maisie took it out and wrapped the egg in it, tying the corners together to form a little bundle. At least it would be safer that way.

Again she turned her attention to the white stone palace.

Had she landed back in Florence?

But no, she decided. Although the enormous white mansion with the columns and balconies looked like it might be in Florence, there was also something very different here. For one thing, Maisie could smell the ocean in the slight breeze. For another, she could just make out high posts topped with gleaming gold eagles off in the distance. And there was so much land stretching out in every direction that Maisie felt certain the city of Florence was nowhere nearby.

In fact, as she dragged the heavy trunk toward the white mansion, she was confident there wasn't a city anywhere around here. The place felt serene, isolated . . . *royal*, Maisie thought.

"Would you like some help with that?" a girl asked.

Maisie looked around but saw no one.

The girl laughed.

"Up here!" she shouted.

Maisie turned her gaze upward until it landed on a girl with strawberry blond hair and a dirty white dress sitting on the high branch of a tree.

"Hello!" Maisie called to her.

"Hello yourself," the girl said, cheekily.

Maisie knew that the royal family had loads of servants, and this girl in the dirty dress must be a servant's daughter. Or perhaps a servant herself.

"So, would you like some help?" the girl asked.

"Yes!" Maisie said.

Maisie watched as she moved to a lower branch and swung from it to another and another until she dropped to the ground, almost directly in front of Maisie.

The girl's cheeks were pink and her blue eyes shiny.

She bowed dramatically.

"At your service," the girl said.

"Thanks," Maisie said. "This thing is heavy."

The girl looked around. "Where's your carriage?" she asked.

"Gone," Maisie answered quickly.

"The footman left without helping you with your trunk?" the girl said, disapprovingly.

Maisie shrugged.

The girl took the handle on the other end of the trunk and hoisted it up, grunting.

"What do you have in here? A body?"

"Just enough clothes to last a while," Maisie answered.

"You're here for the opening party, I assume," the girl said.

"Yes," Maisie said, searching her mind for where she might be. *Not St. Petersburg*, she decided. *It would be colder there. The Finnish coast? No. There would be a yacht, not a mansion.*

She smiled to herself.

Crimea. Definitely. On the Black Sea.

"People are coming from everywhere," the girl said, and Maisie detected a bit of awe in her voice.

"I've come from America," Maisie said, boastfully.

"America!"

The girl paused to study Maisie.

"They don't have royalty there, do they?" she asked, as if that was a very strange thing.

"No. We have a president."

"Does he live in a palace?" the girl asked.

"Not exactly. He lives in the White House," Maisie told her. "But the White House is big." Maisie laughed. "Though not as big as *this* white house."

The girl was delighted with that. "Yes!" she said. "*This* white house has one hundred and sixteen rooms!"

She pointed to the palace.

"All four facades are different," she said. "Isn't that creative?"

The girl took up her end of the trunk again, and she and Maisie continued toward the palace.

"What happened to your king when the government changed?" the girl asked Maisie.

Maisie shuddered, remembering what was going to happen to this royal family.

"We never had a king," she told the girl. "When we became independent from England, we decided to have a president."

"How odd!" the girl said.

When they reached the palace, the girl put down the trunk, motioning for Maisie to do the same.

"I'll get someone to take it from here," she explained.

They walked through a large rose garden, the smell of the flowers so heavy and sweet that it was almost too much to breathe in.

Glass doors led into a large, blindingly white dining room.

Almost immediately a beautiful woman with red-gold hair piled on top of her head and a loose, flowing white dress with lace at her throat and hem swept into the room. At the sight of the girl, she looked horrified.

"Why, you're filthy!" the woman exclaimed.

The girl grinned at her.

"I've climbed almost every tree in the south grove," she said proudly.

"The priests are arriving soon," the woman said. "You must get a bath immediately."

The woman's gaze swept over Maisie.

"And who are you?"

"Maisie Robbins," Maisie said politely, and surprised herself by curtsying.

Maisie produced the letter of introduction and handed it to the woman.

"Yes, yes," she said, barely glancing at it. "We'll get you and your . . ."

Her eyes settled on something written there.

"You and your brother settled," she said.

"You've got a brother?" the girl said happily.

"Felix," Maisie said.

"And where is he?" the woman asked.

Maisie had practically forgotten about Felix. Where was he?

"On his way," she said.

"Fine, fine," the woman said, tossing the letter on the long dining-room table. Above it, an elaborate chandelier glittered in the bright sunlight.

Something caught the woman's attention.

"Is that for me?" she asked, her eyes widening.

Before Maisie could answer, the woman had taken the lace-wrapped Fabergé egg from her.

Slowly, she untied the knot that held the corners together and let the lace fall away to reveal the egg.

"It's lovely!" the woman gasped, holding it up so that the sunlight caught the shine of all the jewels. "And . . . it's made by Fabergé, isn't it?"

Maisie nodded.

"You Americans do bring the most decadent hostess gifts," the woman said. "Thank you. And thank Mr. Pickworth for us."

Who's us? Maisie wondered.

She thought this woman might be the head of the household, in charge of the servants and the kitchen. Surely she should *not* have the egg.

"Does it have a surprise inside?" the woman was asking Maisie.

Maisie swallowed hard. She didn't know whom the egg was for, but the treasure was never for an adult. This woman, whoever she was, couldn't take the egg.

But she was already sweeping back out of the room, saying, "I must show Nikki."

The girl left with her, skipping out the door, and leaving Maisie very much alone.

Someone who clearly was a maid showed Maisie to her room, which was small and plain and disappointing. It did have a little balcony that looked out to the sea, and Maisie stood out there taking in the beautiful view and wondering where Felix had landed. She watched as two footmen carried her trunk inside, and soon enough they knocked at her door and deposited it in her room. Before she'd even finished unlatching it, a maid appeared to unpack for her.

"Oh, that's all right," Maisie said. "I can do it."

She glanced around, and not finding what she needed, asked shyly, "But if you could point me to the ladies' room?"

"Of course, of course," the maid said, and bustled Maisie through a door and into an adjacent bathroom.

When Maisie went back into the bedroom, she found the maid fussing with her clothes after all.

"Shall I prepare your clothes for this evening?" she asked.

"Sure," Maisie said, amused that someone was taking these old clothes so seriously.

The maid gathered a velvet gown and the tiara in her arms, and promised to return to dress Maisie.

"In the meantime," she said, "you should get dressed and meet the others downstairs for the blessing of the house."

Maisie combed her hair, trying to tame it as best she could before going downstairs. She paused on her way at a door that was ajar, revealing several rooms all done in mauve-and-pink chintz. Outside the windows, Maisie saw the ocean and snowcapped mountains.

"Stunning, isn't it?" a man dressed in military clothing asked, startling her.

"Oh!" Maisie said, letting out a little squeal.

The man smiled beneath his big droopy mustache.

"Have you been to this part of the world before?" he asked her.

Maisie shook her head no.

"Unspoiled land," he said, his voice dreamy. "It's been the summer residence for the royal family since the 1860s. But this palace is new, of course."

"It's beautiful," Maisie said.

"Construction took seventeen months, so you can imagine how exciting it is to have it finished at last. And in time for Olga's sixteenth birthday in November, too."

He pulled the door shut and offered his elbow to Maisie.

"Shall we?" he asked.

She felt very grown up and special entering the main rooms below on the arm of this gentle, dashing soldier, dressed in a soft white gown with an empire waist and a satin sash. Maisie hoped that somehow Felix had found his way here and would be downstairs, too.

Everyone's attention was on a group of priests assembling in the dining room. Dressed all in black, with gold cloths over their tunics, very long beards, and very tall hats, the priests stood two by two with the oldest alone at the front. They each held large gold cylinders with holes in them, and even larger crosses. One of the priests set about lighting the incense inside the cylinders, and very quickly the room filled with pungent smoke.

The priests began to sway, swinging the incense back and forth as the leader chanted prayers.

As the priests moved from room to room, leaving a trail of scented smoke behind them, all the guests followed. Maisie kept an eye out for Felix, and for any of the royal family. But the crowd was big enough, and the smoke thick enough, that it was difficult for her to see everyone.

The priests blessed every single room. All one hundred and sixteen.

Maisie thought she might scream with boredom after a while, and as soon as she could, she ducked away from the crowd, backtracking to be sure to avoid running into anyone.

She went through the glass doors she had entered earlier that day, and stepped into the rose garden.

As soon as she did, she heard someone whisper to her.

The same girl who'd been up a tree that afternoon was up another tree here.

"You do like climbing trees," Maisie observed.

"I am going to get in so much trouble if they notice I've slipped away," she said gleefully.

"I guess you like getting in trouble, too," Maisie said.

"I do," the girl agreed. "I'm the naughty one of

OTMA," she added proudly.

Maisie smiled politely. *OTMA?* she thought. The word must not be Russian, or with the shard on she would have understood its meaning.

"It's an acronym, you know," the girl said.

"An acronym?" Maisie repeated.

"A word created from initials," the girl explained.

"*O. T. M. A.*," Maisie said out loud.

"The first letter of each of our names!" the girl announced, climbing even higher in the tree.

"Oh!" she gasped. "From up here I can see the mountains. You should come see!"

Maisie hesitated. She wasn't much of a tree climber.

The girl scampered down far enough to extend her hand and help Maisie onto the lowest branches.

"I don't know," Maisie said, staring up through the leaves into the girl's chubby face.

The girl wiggled her fingers for Maisie to take them.

With a sigh, Maisie relented.

She grabbed on to the girl's hand and let her pull her upward until Maisie got her footing.

Maisie did not like it up there.

"Come on," the girl said, climbing higher.

"I . . . ," Maisie began, but the girl wasn't listening.

Maisie clumsily put her foot into a knot on the bark of the tree, and tried to lift the other foot onto the next branch.

But her foot slipped, and in a second she was dangling from a branch, both legs swinging free.

"Help!" she called.

The last thing she heard was the girl exclaiming, "Hold on!"

Then Maisie's hands let go of the branch, and she plummeted to the ground below.

CHAPTER SIX

ANASTASIA

Maisie lay on her back, staring up at the dappled fading light coming through the leaves of the trees. She was aware of distant voices and footsteps approaching. She was aware of the sharp, constant pain in her right arm. And she was aware of the roses surrounding her, their thorns pricking her cheeks and hands. Maisie had fallen directly into a rosebush.

"Look what you've done now!" a man was saying in a loud stern voice.

The girl with the strawberry blond hair and blue eyes appeared above Maisie.

"She's not dead!" the girl announced, happily.

"That's a relief," came another girl's voice.

Now a second face appeared.

This girl was very pretty, with pink cheeks and brown hair and the biggest blue eyes surrounded by the longest eyelashes that Maisie had ever seen.

"It would be very exciting if she were, though, wouldn't it, Mashka?" the girl asked her.

A third face joined the others.

"Papa has sent for the doctor," she said.

She patted Maisie's hand. "Once," the girl said in a confidential tone, "she put a rock inside a snowball and threw it at me. It hit me right here, in the face, and practically knocked me out."

The girl seemed like a fairy-tale princess to Maisie. Very tall and regal looking, with thick auburn hair and high cheekbones.

"It did knock her down," the first girl said.

"You cried," a fourth voice said, and another face appeared above Maisie.

"No I didn't!" she protested. Then she laughed. "Maybe a little."

The fourth girl was blushing. "What an embarrassment," she said. "To drop a guest out of a tree. Mama had to go lie down she was so upset."

"Hey!" said the first girl, the one whom Maisie had met earlier.

Her face came closer to Maisie's.

"Remember? OTMA?" she asked.

Maisie nodded.

"That's us!" the girl said.

"Olga—" she pointed to the blushing girl.

"Tatiana—" she pointed to the regal one.

"Maria—" she pointed to the pretty one.

The girl grinned impishly.

"And me! Anastasia!"

At that, Maisie burst into tears.

The four Grand Duchesses looked surprised.

"There, there," Olga said.

But Maisie couldn't stop crying. Yes, her arm hurt. A lot. But much worse was the realization that these were the Grand Duchesses, the daughters of Tsar Nicholas and Tsarina Alexandra, and that someday in the near future, they were all doomed to be murdered in the most horrible way.

She thought of the message inside the egg, held out by this very girl in front of her: Anastasia. She had said: HELP ME.

"I do have some good news," Anastasia said, bursting into Maisie's room.

Maisie lay propped up in bed, many pillows behind her head, and her arm resting on even more. After poking it and turning it and moving it every which way, the doctor had declared her arm sprained, not broken. He'd washed the blood from her cheeks and hands where the thorns had pierced her, and then several footmen had lifted her out of the rosebush and up the stairs into bed.

"Your brother has arrived," Anastasia said, flopping onto the bed beside Maisie.

"Don't bounce," Maisie moaned as sharp pains shot through her arm.

"He's very handsome," Anastasia said.

"Where is he?" Maisie asked, eager to see Felix at last.

"The Big Pair has swept him away," Anastasia said unhappily.

"What's the Big Pair?"

Anastasia laughed. "Olga and Tatiana, of course! Mashka and I are the Little Pair because we're the youngest. Except Alexei, of course. But he's a boy."

"Do you think you could bring Felix here?" Maisie asked.

"I suppose," Anastasia said.

She cleared her throat.

"He arrived on horseback with three Tartars. It was so exciting!"

Maisie frowned. Tartars?

"The local people," Anastasia explained when she saw the confusion on Maisie's face. "They invaded Russia hundreds of years ago, but of course we conquered them under Catherine the Great, and now their allegiance is to Papa instead of their khans."

Before Maisie could answer, Anastasia smiled. "I love them," she said. "The women are beautiful. They cover their faces with veils and look so mysterious. And the men are so dashing!"

Unsure of how to respond, Maisie smiled back.

"So? You'll get Felix?" she reminded Anastasia.

"Happily!" Anastasia said, and bounced off the bed, sending new sharp pains through Maisie's arm.

Before Maisie could reprimand her, Anastasia was out the door, running down the hallway and shouting, "Olga! Tatiana!"

"Darling," a man said gently, "Mama is resting. And so is Alexei."

A knock sounded at the bedroom door, and when Maisie called, "Come in," the man who had escorted her downstairs earlier entered.

He had a tray with a bowl of steaming soup on it and a glass of tea. Maisie remembered that Alex Andropov's grandmother had served tea that way too, in a glass instead of a cup.

"A little soup always nourishes the sick," the man said.

When he placed the tray on the table beside the bed, a sour smell floated toward Maisie.

"What kind of soup is this?" she asked, trying to sound polite.

"Cabbage," the man said, smiling, as if that were the best soup in the world.

Maisie nodded, but didn't pick up the silver spoon that rested beside the bowl.

"We haven't met properly," the man was saying. "What with the blessing and then your accident . . . well, it's been a little busy around here."

"Maisie Robbins," she said. "Phinneas Pickworth is my—"

"Yes," he said, "Sunny told me. We adore Phinneas. Such a character! Such . . . such an American!"

What an odd thing to say, Maisie thought.

"Well, Maisie, eat your soup and rest up. And please forgive Anastasia. She's a bit rambunctious, that's all."

He turned to leave, but Maisie said, "But you haven't told me who you are."

The man laughed.

"Why, I'm the Tsar. Tsar Nicholas," he said shyly.

"You're the Tsar?" Maisie said, shocked.

He stood no more than five feet eight, and had such a shy, sad smile and such gentle eyes that she couldn't imagine why anyone would fear him or want to overthrow his government.

"I'm afraid so," Tsar Nicholas admitted.

"Of all of Russia?" Maisie asked.

He laughed again. "All of it," he said.

"But you're so nice!" she said. "I thought Tsars were tall and fierce."

Tsar Nicholas considered this.

"I suppose some have been," he said, finally.

Maisie's mind was racing.

"Then that beautiful woman with the auburn hair is the Empress?" she asked, just to be sure.

"She is beautiful, isn't she?" he said softly.

"This wasn't at all what I expected," Maisie said, thinking of Bolsheviks and conquering Tsars and all sorts of scary things.

"That's good," the Tsar said. "I think?"

"Oh yes," Maisie said. "It's good."

"Now you must get better," the Tsar said as he headed toward the door. "Next week is Easter, and you don't want to be stuck in this bed during Easter, do you?"

It must have been a rhetorical question because he left without even pausing for Maisie's answer.

Felix recognized the chubby girl with the strawberry blond hair and blue eyes immediately.

"Grand Duchess Anastasia," he said, and gave a curt bow.

Anastasia giggled.

"Felix Robbins," Felix continued, liking the way her face lit up when she laughed.

"Oh!" Anastasia squealed. "You're Maisie's brother!"

Her demeanor changed quickly.

"Don't be angry at me," she said. "Please, please, please."

Angry? Felix thought. He didn't think he could

be angry with this girl. Something about her made him just want to grin.

"I didn't know she was so clumsy," Anastasia said, her voice stubborn now. "I didn't *make* her climb that tree."

"Maisie is okay, isn't she?" Felix asked.

"Oh no!" Anastasia said, and burst into tears.

"Isn't she?" Felix asked again.

"It's her fault! I swear to you!"

And at that, Anastasia placed her hand over her heart dramatically.

Then she laughed again.

"It's just her arm," Anastasia said, dismissively.

"Broken?" Felix asked with dread.

"Not even! She's absolutely fine. By Easter she'll be . . . she'll be climbing trees again!"

Felix sighed with relief.

Then a thought came to him.

"When's Easter?" he asked.

"Next week, silly!" Anastasia said, linking her arm through his. "Come on now. I'll bring you to this invalid sister of yours."

Despite her relief at seeing Felix here, Maisie was not happy to see Anastasia this time.

"I can't believe you let me go," she said, angrily.

"I can't believe you couldn't climb even one branch," Anastasia countered.

"Maisie cannot climb trees," Felix said, laughing softly. "At all."

Maisie glared at him, her relief at finding him in front of her safe and fine fading.

"Whose side are you on, anyway?" she demanded.

"Side?" Felix said. "I didn't know there were sides. I just know that you don't know how to climb trees—"

"See!" Anastasia said with so much delight that Maisie glared harder. "It's all your own fault!"

Maisie closed her eyes.

"I need to rest," she said. "The Tsar insists."

Anastasia laughed at that.

"That's Papa!" she said. "Tsar Nicholas II!"

"Anastasia!" Grand Duchess Tatiana said from the doorway. "Mama would not like to hear you bragging like this."

Anastasia's cheeks blushed pink.

"I wasn't bragging," she muttered. "Governess," she added under her breath.

Tatiana tugged playfully on Anastasia's hair.

"That old nickname is not going to upset me, Malenkaya," she said.

"I'm not little." Anastasia pouted. "Don't call me that."

Felix studied Grand Duchess Tatiana. Tall and slender, she had such grace and poise that he found himself speechless beside her. Speechless in a different way than Anastasia made him feel.

"Papa wants to be sure our guest has eaten all of her soup," Tatiana said, crossing to the bed.

She glanced down at the tray.

"Why, you haven't even touched it!" she clucked. "And now it's gone cold."

Tatiana picked up the tray and said, "I'll bring you a fresh bowl."

"No!" Maisie said, half-sitting.

Tatiana looked surprised.

"I mean, no thank you. I just want to sleep for a bit."

Maisie would have liked to tell Felix that the soup was cabbage soup and therefore disgusting, but he wasn't even looking at her. Instead, he was gazing at that horrid Anastasia.

"All right, then," Tatiana was saying. "Then we'll leave you for a bit."

"Felix," Maisie said. "I do need to tell you something." She shot a look at Anastasia. "In private," she added.

"What?" he asked, even though they were most definitely not in private.

Maisie beckoned him to come close.

"What?" he asked again, closer but still in earshot of Anastasia.

"I need to whisper it to you," Maisie said, frustrated.

Anastasia said, "Telling secrets in front of others is rude."

Felix hesitated, but Maisie yanked him nearer.

"The Empress has the egg," she whispered.

"The Empress has—" he began.

"Ssshhh!" Maisie hushed.

"But why does she have it?" Felix whispered back.

"It doesn't matter," Maisie said. "You have to find where she put it and take it back."

"I'm leaving right now," Anastasia announced.

"I'm coming!" Felix said quickly.

But Maisie held on to his arm.

"Promise?" she said.

"Okay," he said, shrugging her off.

"Do you want to write a play?" Anastasia asked Felix. "Then we can perform it for Mama and Papa."

"Yes!" Felix said, ignoring Maisie's attempts to get his attention. "I love writing plays."

"I have the lead in the school play," Maisie said.

But Tatiana was already out the door, and Anastasia had linked arms with Felix again and was babbling about her big idea for a play, and Felix was nodding his head like a bobblehead doll.

"The lead!" Maisie shouted after them.

Anastasia turned toward Maisie ever so slightly, and—Maisie was certain—smirked at her!

"Hey!" Maisie said as Anastasia pulled the door firmly shut behind her.

"Harumph," Maisie said, snuggling deeper into the fluffy white duvet.

She did not like Anastasia Romanov. Not one bit.

❄️

Much later that night, Maisie was awoken by a sound.

"Psssstttt."

Maisie pulled the duvet up snugger around her.

"Psssstttt."

What was that noise?

She opened her eyes and found the room swaddled in darkness. Except the light from the full moon that came in one window.

"Pssssttttt," she heard again.

The sound was coming from the closet.

Maisie frowned.

"Maisie," came the voice from the closet. "Can you open the door? There's no handle in here."

"No," Maisie said, trying to sound brave even though she was trembling, "I will not open the closet and let a stranger out."

"I'm not a stranger," the voice said.

"Go away!" Maisie shouted. Panicked, her eyes searched the dark room for a weapon of some kind.

On the wall hung an ornate religious picture made of silver. It looked heavy enough to bop someone on the head good and hard, Maisie decided.

"Maisie," the voice said again.

As quietly as she could, Maisie inched her way off the bed.

"Ouch!" she blurted, forgetting how badly her arm hurt.

"Your arm?" the voice said.

How did this person know about her arm?

Maisie tiptoed over to the wall and, with her good hand, lifted the picture from its place there. She looked down into the face of a holy-looking woman holding a baby, blue jewels sparkling in halos above their heads and Cyrillic letters written beneath them. To her satisfaction, the picture was pretty heavy.

"Maisie?" the voice said again.

"I'm coming," Maisie said, hoping her voice didn't betray her fear.

How did a person get into the closet in the first place? And how did the person know her name? Something was very weird here.

Although it hurt a lot, she turned the knob of the closet door with the hand of her sprained arm, and lifted the icon up high with her good one.

She heard a rustling from the closet, and then a figure stepped out into the dark room.

Maisie brought the icon down as hard as she could on his head.

With a loud grunt, the figure fell to the floor.

Shaking, Maisie looked down into the face of Alex Andropov.

CHAPTER SEVEN

EASTER

"Alex Andropov!" Maisie gasped.

"Why did you hit me?" Alex groaned, rubbing his head.

"I didn't know it was you hiding in my closet," Maisie said.

Alex grinned up at Maisie.

"I knew when you spoke perfect Russian that there was something peculiar going on," he said.

"Of course, I had no idea you were . . . time traveling," he added, his eyes sweeping over the room.

"But how did you get here?" Maisie asked, still not quite able to believe that Alex Andropov was standing in her room at the Livadia Palace.

He pointed his thumb over his shoulder.

"Your trunk," he said, obviously proud of himself.

Maisie remembered how the things in the trunk had appeared to shift when she'd opened it earlier. She remembered how heavy it was when she'd dragged it here. Alex had been inside the whole time.

"I got a little worried when that maid wanted to unpack it for you," Alex chuckled. "But when she showed you to the bathroom, I climbed out and hid. Just in the nick of time, too, I might add."

"But you're not a Pickworth," Maisie said, confused.

"What's a Pickworth?"

"Phinneas Pickworth collected all of the items that allow us to time travel," Maisie explained. "But you need to be related to him in order to do it."

Alex shrugged. "Well," he said, "here I am."

"And you have to be a twin!" Maisie said, even more confused.

"Well," Alex said again, "I'm not."

"It doesn't make sense," Maisie insisted.

"You hit me with a religious icon, you know," he said, pointing to the silver icon Maisie still held.

"Probably a very valuable one, too."

Alex stood at the window and stared out.

"We're at the palace in Livadia, aren't we?" he asked, his voice soft and reverential.

"Yes," Maisie answered.

Slowly, he turned to face her.

"I can't believe they were in here. Anastasia and Tatiana. And the Tsar himself."

"And I can't believe you're in here," Maisie said, unhappily.

Alex sat on the edge of the bed, looking thoughtful.

"Tell me," he said. "Do you just come here? Is that why you speak Russian?"

Maisie didn't feel like explaining The Treasure Chest to Alex. In fact, she didn't feel like talking to him at all.

"It's complicated," she said.

"Can you try to explain?" he persisted.

"Later," she said. "For now, my arm hurts and I'm supposed to have it elevated."

"But where should I go?" Alex asked.

"How should I know?" Maisie snapped. "You're not even supposed to be here!"

Thankfully, Felix knocked on her door just then.

"Who are you talking to in there?" he whispered.

He opened the door and started to enter the room. But as soon as he saw Alex Andropov, he stopped in his tracks.

"What are you doing here?" Felix said, his eyes wide with surprise.

"He hid inside the trunk!" Maisie said.

Alex grinned at Maisie and Felix.

"And he's not even a twin," Maisie said, "never mind a Pickworth!"

Felix closed the door behind him.

"I guess he's stuck here now," Felix said.

"Stuck?" Alex said, his eyes bright. "I've never been so happy in my life! I'm in my homeland, with my ancestors!"

"Take him to your room," Maisie suggested. "I've got to get some sleep."

"But how will I explain who he is?" Felix asked, exasperated.

"No need for you to explain anything," Alex said. "I can explain my lineage to the Tsar myself. I will be welcome here as a Romanov."

Felix was considering something. Maisie could

tell by the way he scrunched up his face.

"You know," he said, "somehow James Ferocious came back with us from Amelia Earhart's—"

"Amelia Earhart!" Alex interrupted. "So you time travel everywhere?"

Maisie waited for Felix to answer him.

But Alex kept talking.

"Have you met Julius Caesar?" Alex asked eagerly. "King Tut? George Washington?"

Felix ignored him.

"I never thought about it before, but technically James Ferocious shouldn't have been able to come back with us. I mean he's not a Pickworth."

"That's true," Maisie said.

"But when I tried to bring Lily Goldberg with me, it didn't work," Felix said, remembering when he took Lily up to The Treasure Chest.

"There's something we don't understand, then," Maisie agreed. "Because James Ferocious is at Elm Medona, and Alex Andropov is right here, right now."

"Yes, he is," Felix said.

Alex puffed his chest out, obviously delighted with himself.

"Well," Maisie said, slowly, forgetting for an instant about the problem of Alex Andropov. "We brought James Ferocious back with us. Like when we got back from Hawaii, I found a seashell in my pocket."

Felix nodded, thinking hard.

"Alex was in the trunk," he said. "I guess that's all it took."

Maisie looked sad. "If we had known that, we could have taken Great-Uncle Thorne with us."

"Enough!" Alex said angrily. "Take me to the Tsar."

"Now?" Felix asked. "It's the middle of the night!"

"I'll tell him I just arrived," Alex said.

Felix sighed.

"I'll bring you to Olga. She'll know what to do," he told Alex.

Maisie watched Felix and Alex leave. Then she got back in bed. But she couldn't go to sleep. She stared at the full moon hanging over the Black Sea until dawn broke, and finally, sleep came.

Olga seemed taken by Alex's story. "A long-lost cousin!" she said with delight.

But she refused to bother Papa with it that night. Instead, she showed Alex to a guest room, and brought him down to breakfast with her and the other Duchesses the next morning.

When Alex explained to the Tsar over breakfast who he was related to, the Tsar jumped to his feet and wrapped Alex in a big bear hug. Soon, Alex was joining the entire royal family on their morning swim in the sea.

Almost the entire family.

For most of that first week, Felix did not see the Empress or little Alexei, the Tsarevich. When he asked Anastasia about them she grew evasive.

"Oh, Mama likes to spend private time with him," she'd say.

Or: "They have their own routines."

Routines were the way of life here, Felix quickly learned.

Every morning, after a breakfast of bread and butter, everyone except the Empress and Alexei went swimming in the sea. Usually, the Tsar followed that with tennis while the Grand Duchesses knit or sewed or read until lunchtime. Lunch was the big meal, with a lavish spread of suckling pig, caviar, whole fish and smoked fish, soup, and fruit set out. After lunch, they went for long walks in the woods, always collecting treasures—twigs, nests, mushrooms, berries, flowers—for the Empress. Then it was teatime, followed by performances of the plays the girls wrote, or piano concerts, or poetry recitals. Supper was served late at night, and afterward everyone went off to bed.

The routine rarely changed, although a few times the Tsar took everyone by horseback to nearby villas. Felix found the sameness of the days comforting, and easily adapted to them. But he found himself more and more looking forward to those moments when he could be with Anastasia, writing little skits or just walking together on the grounds. By the end of the week, Felix knew that he had a big-time crush on Anastasia. And by the way she blushed when he spoke to her, or good-naturedly teased him, he thought she had a crush on him, too.

Meanwhile, Maisie spent all her time recovering in bed. Sometimes she heard the Empress and the Tsarevich talking together on the Empress's balcony, their laughter carrying in the breeze. By the end of the week, Maisie began to sit on her little balcony every afternoon. From there she would see the Empress driving a cart pulled by a pony around the grounds, or wandering in the gardens. She looked sad, Maisie decided. How could someone live in this beautiful palace, surrounded by such a big and loving family, and look so sad?

But even as she wondered this, Maisie realized the answer. Little Alexei suffered from hemophilia. And that was the source of the Empress's great sorrow.

At home, Easter used to be an egg hunt at the playground, Easter baskets filled with hot-pink and neon-green plastic grass with chocolate bunnies tucked inside, and a special brunch out somewhere nicer than the corner diner. No matter where they went, Maisie and Felix's father always got eggs Benedict, his fancy brunch order. The rest of them tried the restaurant's specialties, or something extra special like stuffed French toast or house-made sausage or crepes. They would pass families wearing Easter outfits—kids in matching clothes or women in big hats. But after brunch, they just went home and got back in their pajamas and played rounds of charades or hearts until their mother finally announced it was time to watch the old movie *Easter Parade*. Maisie and Felix groaned and complained, but eventually they got caught up in Judy Garland and Fred Astaire singing "A Couple of Swells" and the big finale of the song "Easter Parade."

Their father could be counted on to do a terrible imitation of Peter Lawford singing "A Fella with an Umbrella," and their mother could be counted on to beg him to stop, which he wouldn't. That was Easter at 10 Bethune Street.

Easter at Livadia Palace was an entirely different occasion, and Felix watched with great interest as the household prepared for the celebration.

Anastasia explained to him that in Russia, Easter was even more important and more fun than Christmas.

"More fun than Christmas?" Felix said in disbelief. "That's impossible!"

"You'll see," she promised.

❋

For several afternoons before Easter, Felix and Alex joined the four Grand Duchesses to make Easter eggs.

"Wow!" Felix said when he first saw some of the

complicated, intricately decorated eggs. "At home we just stick hard-boiled eggs in dye!"

Alex gave a look of disgust.

"Some of us do," he said. "Other families make traditional Easter eggs."

Suddenly, he seemed very sad.

"What's the matter, Alex?" Felix asked him.

"I'm so happy to be here," Alex said wistfully. "But I miss my babushka. You see, both of my parents died when I was very young, and it's just been Babushka and me for most of my life."

"Your parents died?" Felix asked. "Both of them?"

Alex nodded.

"It was very sad, of course. But I was too young to even remember them. Babushka and I decorated traditional eggs every Easter. She makes the most beautiful eggs you can imagine."

"You'll be back with her in no time," Felix said.

To his surprise, Alex's face changed completely, from sadness to resolve.

"We shall see," Alex said, turning his attention back to the egg he was painting.

Olga's hand on his arm brought Felix's attention back to the others at the table.

"I will teach you," Olga said.

Olga showed Felix the tools he would need to use.

"These are the *kistkas*," she said, picking up three different things that resembled pencils, but with wooden handles and copper tips. Each one was a different thickness.

"We just heat the tip over the candle like this," Olga continued, demonstrating. "And when it's heated through we hold it gently against the beeswax."

Felix watched her as she filled the *kistka* with the melted beeswax.

"Now I can draw my designs," she explained.

"You are forgetting one very important detail," Anastasia said.

"What's that?" Olga asked, concentrating on her decorating.

Alex laughed. "I think I know!"

Anastasia picked up a white egg from a basket at the end of the table, and a pin from a pincushion beside it.

Carefully, Anastasia poked the shell at the broadest end of the egg with the pin, then she inserted the pin enough so that she could mix the yolk into the egg whites. She took another pin and pierced the other end of the shell with it.

"You should let Felix do it," Tatiana said, her eyes merry.

"I'm not going to eat a raw egg," Felix said.

"You don't eat it!" Alex said.

Anastasia laughed. "Watch," she said, picking up a straw and holding it over the small hole.

She took a deep breath and blew, hard, sending egg guts out the other end.

"Anastasia!" Olga said. "You're supposed to do that over the bowl."

"Oops!" Anastasia said, unapologetically.

Maria held up a finished egg for Felix to see. It was black with large yellow flowers, red berries, and delicate green leaves painted on it.

"It's beautiful," Felix said.

"My babushka's eggs are even more beautiful," Alex said.

Maria added it to the basket of other eggs: deep purple ones with green, red, and blue geometric designs; black with yellow and red bees; red swirls with gold; light blue with white scrolls . . . a display of color and design like Felix had never seen before.

He couldn't help but think of the spotty pink, blue, and green eggs his family had dyed when he and Maisie were very little. His mother bought a kit from the drugstore and dropped tablets of dye in paper cups with water and white vinegar. They all wrote their names with a crayon on the egg, the name appearing as the dye took hold. The entire process took about twenty minutes, and then for the next week they had egg salad tinged blue, or deviled eggs with pink around the filling, which Felix refused to eat.

These Easter eggs were exciting to make and beautiful to look at. *Maisie would love making them, too*, he thought. But when he invited her to come downstairs the next afternoon, she refused.

"I don't want to be a third wheel," she said, huffily.

"What are you talking about?" Felix asked, confused. "Everyone's doing it together in the salon. OTMA and—"

"Oh! It's OTMA now, is it?" Maisie said, rolling her eyes.

Of course Felix had gotten all cozy with the Grand Duchesses while she lay in bed recuperating. *Just like in school*, Maisie thought with a familiar pang. Everyone loved Felix, and she was an interloper.

"That's just what they call themselves," Felix explained.

"I don't even like dyeing Easter eggs," Maisie said. "We used to do it, you know. When we were little."

"Of course I remember that," Felix said kindly. "But this is different."

He held out one of the eggs he'd decorated.

"Look," he said. "I made this one for you."

Maisie frowned at the fancy egg in his hand. It was the prettiest shade of blue and covered with white flowers that had red centers and a trellis of pale green leaves running around it.

"You made that?" she said, even more miserable now.

Somehow Felix had learned to make these gorgeous eggs, and if she went downstairs everyone would be decorating eggs, except her. She wouldn't have a clue where to begin.

As if he'd read her mind, Felix said, "I'll teach you how to do it. It's really not too hard. You should see the ones Alex made. And you get to blow the yolks out of a tiny hole in the egg! That part is really fun."

That part did sound like fun, Maisie had to

admit. But still, she was tired of always being the one who walked into a group that was friends, having to prove herself somehow.

"Maybe tomorrow," she said, and closed her eyes to signal the conversation was over.

After she heard Felix leave, she opened her eyes again.

He'd placed the decorated egg on the table beside the bed. When Maisie picked it up, she was surprised how light it was, as if it weren't an egg at all.

❄

"I think," Anastasia said, her voice low, "this one is the most beautiful of all."

Felix watched as she took a Fabergé egg down from a mantel on which a dozen others sat. This egg was blue, green, and yellow, with thin silver lines running across it.

Anastasia traced the silver lines.

"This is Siberia," she said, "and these lines are the route of the railroad."

"Wow," Felix said, impressed.

"Papa was the chairman of the railway committee that built the Great Siberian Railway," Anastasia explained.

"Isn't he the chairman of everything?" Felix asked.

Anastasia looked delighted.

"I suppose he is!" she said.

She sat cross-legged on the floor and patted the spot beside her for Felix to sit.

When he did, she said, "Mr. Fabergé made this in 1900, to commemorate the railroad."

Anastasia touched the golden two-headed eagle at the top of the egg, and to Felix's surprise the top lifted.

"Look," Anastasia said, excited to show him the surprise inside.

Felix could not believe what he saw when he did as she asked.

Inside was a train with five cars and a locomotive, all of it only about a foot long and less than an inch wide.

"It's the Siberian Express!" Anastasia said with delight, clapping her hands together.

She held up a gold key.

"Play with it," she told Felix, handing him the key.

"Really?" he asked.

Anastasia nodded and Felix turned the key, illuminating the diamond that made the headlights of the gold and silver locomotive.

"Turn it again!" Anastasia said, excitedly.

When Felix did, the locomotive began to pull the five cars.

"That's the baggage car, and the ladies car, and that one is our car!" she explained, pointing as each moved past.

"And the one with the cross is the church car," she continued. "See the gold bells on the roof?"

"This is amazing!" Felix said.

Miss Landers had told the class to only say *awesome* when something truly inspired awe, and to only say *amazing* when one was truly amazed. He decided this was the kind of thing that earned both awesome and amazing.

From the mantel, the top of another egg flew open and a bejeweled rooster emerged on a platform, flapping its wings and crowing.

Felix stared at it.

"Awesome!" he said.

As he watched the rooster sink back down into the egg, his eye caught sight of something familiar.

There on the mantel, with all the other Fabergé eggs, sat the one he and Maisie had brought with them.

Now that he had found it, he just had to figure out how to get it back.

✻

"What's your problem?" Alex Andropov asked Maisie.

His nose was peeling and his cheeks were pink from sunburn.

"I don't remember inviting you into my room," Maisie said. "In fact, I don't remember inviting you to Russia!"

Rather than getting angry or offended, Alex smiled at Maisie.

"Easter begins tonight," he said. "It's the most important celebration of the year."

"So?"

"So you have to get out of bed and celebrate," Alex said patiently. "Aunt Alex—"

"She's your aunt now? The Empress?"

"She's always been my aunt," he reminded Maisie. "And she's worked tirelessly to prepare for Easter here, and you need to show up."

Maisie sighed. "I know," she mumbled.

Alex sat on the edge of her bed, looking worried.

"What's wrong? I mean, other than your arm?"

"My arm is actually better," Maisie admitted.

"Then what?"

"For some reason, I always get left out," Maisie said. "And now if I show up, everyone will have private jokes and know things I don't know and . . . they even have memories together already that I'll never share."

Saying it out loud made her worries seem dumb.

"I know it's dumb," Maisie said.

Alex laughed softly.

"I don't think it's dumb at all," he said. "I feel that way all the time. I miss so much school, and when I'm there I never know what anyone's talking about or what's going on in class. That's why I got so excited when you said you were interested in Imperial Russia," he added, his cheeks growing pinker. "I thought, *Finally someone who likes something I like.*"

Alex had been looking down at the floor as he spoke. But now he looked at Maisie.

"Now *that* sounds dumb," he said.

"No!" Maisie said. "No! I get it! I do!"

"Will you come to the Easter celebration if I

promise to stick by your side? I'll be sure you won't feel left out," Alex said.

Maisie couldn't say no.

"All right," she said. "But if you go off with a Grand Duchess or two and leave me behind, you'll be sorry."

"The festivities start at midnight," Alex said, heading toward the door.

"Midnight?" Maisie repeated to herself.

❋

Alex stayed true to his word. He even explained all the traditions to her.

"Imagine," he said, his eyes shining, "all across Russia everyone is doing these very things."

Maisie thought of how big Russia was, spreading across the wall in the Map Room at Elm Medona. *It's impressive*, she thought, *that cathedrals and houses everywhere in this enormous country are saying the same prayers and eating these same foods.*

Eating seemed to be a very important part of Easter here. All night and the next morning, the Tsar and Tsarina hosted hundreds of people, serving food from enormous tables and giving their guests three kisses.

"One for blessing," Alex explained, "one for welcome, and one for joy."

He brought Maisie extra helpings of the creamy dessert she liked, and also made sure she tasted the Easter cake topped with white frosting. He even tried to teach her a Russian dance that involved lots of kicking and spinning, but Maisie's legs got tangled together, and she got so dizzy trying to keep up with Alex when she spun around that she knocked into two other dancers. Usually, something like that would make her feel embarrassed, but the dancers and Alex just laughed good-naturedly. "Maybe no more spinning," Alex said. Instead, he concentrated on trying to teach her the secret to such rapid kicking.

Even though Maisie had a good time, she hardly saw Felix during the entire celebration. He was swept away by Anastasia, sending Maisie a wave across the banquet table and a shrug as he helped hand out Easter eggs to the schoolchildren of Yalta who filed in the next morning. If it wasn't for Alex Andropov, Maisie decided, she would have had another terrible time, and Felix would have been clueless, as usual.

When the festivities were finally over and

everyone went to rest, Felix passed Maisie in the hallway. He was, of course, following Anastasia.

"Wasn't that great?" he asked Maisie.

He didn't wait for her to answer. He just kept walking.

"It was great!" Maisie shouted after him.

Anastasia turned and grinned at Maisie.

"Just wait until we leave for Finland next month," she said. "That's lots of fun, too."

Finland? There was no way, Maisie decided right then and there, that she was sticking around long enough to go to Finland.

CHAPTER EIGHT

ALEX ANDROPOV'S THREAT

But Maisie had never been more wrong in her life. She and Felix did board the Imperial yacht, *Standart*, along with Alex Andropov and the entire royal family. Even though Felix looked anxious, Maisie decided to stay mad at him. Anastasia and Maria were both stuck to him like Velcro, so Maisie explored the yacht by herself.

The decks were all white—awnings, wicker tables, wicker chairs.

Maisie went below, wandering through dozens of rooms with rich wood paneling and sparkling chandeliers.

"Oh! Excuse me," murmured a man who bumped into her with his trumpet case.

"Pardon me," said a man right behind him. This man carried an enormous tuba case.

"Pardon," said the next man. He held a strange-shaped instrument in his hand. It had a long neck and a triangle-shaped body with just three strings.

"What is that?" Maisie asked him.

The man looked at her as if she were either crazy or dumb. "A balalaika," he said, reminding Maisie of how Great-Uncle Thorne sounded when she and Felix didn't know something that he thought was completely obvious.

"Where are you all going?" she asked another man with a balalaika.

"To our rooms," he answered. "Below."

"You're going to Finland?" she asked. "An entire orchestra?"

"Just the brass," he said. "And the balalaikas," he added, holding up his.

Maisie continued her exploration, having to stop again for what appeared to be the Royal Army, and then again when Olga came rushing up to her.

"We've been looking everywhere for you!" Olga said, breathlessly. "You need to meet your sailor."

"*My* sailor?" Maisie said as Olga pulled her along.

"We each get one," Olga said. "They're divine. Really lovely."

Maisie glimpsed what appeared to be the Imperial Navy fleet surrounding the yacht.

"Are they coming from there?" she asked Olga.

Olga barely glanced at the ships.

"No, no," she said. "They just escort our ship."

At Livadia, it had been easy to forget just how imperial the Imperial Family was. But rushing along the *Standart* that morning to meet her own personal sailor, with the army and the navy fleet and the orchestra, Maisie realized that she was in the presence of something she'd never experienced before. And in that moment, she began to understand why the people of Russia began a revolution.

It seemed to Felix that Maisie was obsessed with just how imperial the Imperial Family was. The size of their yacht. The personal sailors for the Grand Duchesses. The balalaika orchestra. The navy escort. All of it made her feel that maybe the people of Russia were not getting fair treatment. After all, she argued, if the Tsar had so much, what did everyone else have?

Felix tried to listen. He really did.

But he had other things on his mind.

First of all, he liked Anastasia. A lot. And all this complaining about the royal family made him uneasy.

And second of all, the egg that they'd brought with them was sitting on a mantel back at Livadia. Which meant they could not go back home. Even if they wanted to. Which, Felix had to admit, was something he most certainly did not want. Still, he knew from experience that he might *have* to go home. Anything could happen at any time, sending them headlong into danger.

Felix knew they needed that egg.

But he decided not to tell Maisie where it was. She was so worried about injustices to the people of Russia, she appeared to have forgotten all about the egg anyway.

Even though Felix enjoyed his time on the *Standart*, spending his days much as he did at Livadia—walking in the woods or on the beach, writing and performing plays, sleeping under a starlit sky—he did wonder when they might go back to Crimea.

The Empress's friend Anna Vyrubova had joined

them, and she and the Empress spent much of their time together knitting or playing the piano. The sounds of Tchaikovsky often filled the afternoon air. They did appear at teatime, and listened to the music of the brass band or the balalaika orchestra as the Grand Duchesses showed them the things they'd collected on their walks.

"They lead a boring life," Maisie whispered to Felix one day after they'd been cruising along the Finnish coast for a few weeks.

"It's not boring," he said. "It's just different from ours, that's all."

Maisie rolled her eyes.

"I bet the Russian people are out working in fields and factories while their leaders collect sea glass," she said with a huff.

One day the Dowager Empress arrived via her yacht, *Polar Star*, and that was the excitement for the next forty-eight hours. The Dowager Empress had been the empress before her husband, Tsar Alexander, died suddenly. She hardly ever lived in Russia anymore, and everyone was all excited to have her aboard.

The only person who didn't appear was Alexei.

He stayed in his room, or with his mother, out of sight.

When the Dowager Empress was aboard, Maisie saw her go into the Tsarevich's stateroom, but try as she might, Maisie couldn't catch a glimpse of the boy.

After two months cruising around the fjords of Finland, Anastasia announced to Felix that they were leaving the *Standart*.

"Back to Livadia?" he asked hopefully.

"No," she told him. "We spend August in our hunting lodge in Poland."

And so on they went to Spala, the Imperial hunting lodge in the heart of Bialowieza Primeval Forest. They arrived there on September 1, riding in a line of grand carriages, each drawn by two horses dressed in fancy headgear. In Newport, the mansions were called *cottages* by their original owners. Spala was kind of like that, an enormous mansion that the royal family called a *hunting lodge*.

When they walked inside, Felix gasped. The walls of the entry hall were covered with animal heads. The heads stared down at them with glassy yellow eyes, the antlers and horns jutting from the tops.

"You mean you really hunt here?" Felix asked, trying not to make eye contact with any of the dead animals staring at him.

Anastasia laughed. "*We* don't, silly. Papa does."

She began pointing to each head and naming what it was. *Or what it had been*, Felix thought, feeling even creepier.

"Stag. Stag. Bison. Boar. Auroch—"

"Thanks," Felix said, relieved to follow everyone up to the second-floor bedrooms.

But before he even got to the stairs, the Tsar stopped him and Alex Andropov.

"Would you two like to join us on the hunt tomorrow morning?" the Tsar asked.

"Yes!" Alex said enthusiastically.

At the same time Felix said, "No!" just as enthusiastically.

"Wonderful," the Tsar said. "We leave at eight in the morning."

He patted each boy on the head before he moved to help his wife upstairs.

"Hunting at Spala," Alex said dreamily.

"But, Alex, I don't want to go hunting."

Alex didn't seem to hear him. He was too busy

gazing up at those heads on the wall.

"Twenty-eight points," Alex said.

Tatiana paused. "Yes," she said. "What a trophy! Twenty-eight points on that stag's antlers. It was shot by Prince Kotchube, one of the best shots in the world."

"Is he coming with us tomorrow?" Felix asked, not sure if that would be a good thing or a bad thing.

Tatiana shook her head.

"Hurry, now," she said. "Papa is getting the diamond!"

Happy to leave those heads, Felix ran up the stairs, catching up with Maisie.

"Happy hunting," she teased him.

Felix could only groan.

They joined the others in the Tsar's study. The centerpiece of the room was an enormous oak desk, stretching at least seven feet across. Around the room were many couches made out of oak trees.

Anastasia saw Felix looking at them and whispered, "Those trees were a thousand years old."

"And you cut them down to make couches?" Felix asked in disbelief.

"This forest is full of trees that old," Anastasia

explained. "There's one that's over twelve hundred years old."

The Tsar cleared his throat. He was standing at the window holding a large diamond that sparkled in the afternoon sun.

Once everyone had gathered, the Tsar began etching something into the window with the diamond. The sound reminded Felix of fingernails on a chalkboard, and he shivered.

"What's he doing?" Maisie asked.

Maria answered her in a quiet voice. "When we arrive, he etches the date we arrived in the window with that diamond. Isn't it a lovely tradition?"

Maisie thought it was kind of weird, but by this time, with entire orchestras on the yacht and personal sailors, nothing the royal family did surprised her.

The next morning promptly at eight, cars arrived to take the hunters into the forest. Felix had barely been able to eat the night before as they sat in the dining room that seated one hundred and fifty people, eating a sumptuous dinner of wild boar and pheasant. This morning he couldn't even manage to eat the usual basic breakfast of bread and butter and tea. His stomach was tied up in knots, and all he could think of as they got deeper and deeper into the forest was how he could escape without getting mistaken for a stag himself.

The Tsar told Felix and Alex Andropov that they would stay with him, in the center. He helped them hide in the foliage, and when he saw the look of terror on Felix's face, he kneeled so that they were eye to eye.

"Felix," the Tsar said softly, "I don't love hunting or killing. For me, this is a chance to be outdoors in this beautiful forest. And I think you are like me. You don't want to hunt. You just want to enjoy nature and this glorious day. So stand right here beside me, and do just that."

"Thank you," Felix said, relieved.

The sound of a trumpet interrupted them, followed by the commander of the hunt's order to begin.

Immediately, the forest grew noisy with shouts and cracks, the sounds echoing in the quiet.

Directly in front of Felix, Alex, and the Tsar, a herd of stag ran past. Felix squeezed his eyes shut, not wanting to see these beautiful animals hurt.

But then he heard the Tsar say, "Let's just watch

these majestic animals pass, shall we?"

Felix cracked his eyes open enough to see just that.

In front of the stags, a herd of wild boar ran past, snorting. And beyond, a red fox walked slowly by.

Felix could feel his heart beating in his chest. But not with fear. Instead, he was filled with an admiration and wonder at the beauty of nature.

When they broke for lunch, which was served on a long table draped in fine linen with gold-and-silver plates, Felix thanked the Tsar.

"Me?" the Tsar said. "I didn't create this magnificent place. I only shared it with you."

For the rest of their time at Spala, even though Alex Andropov eagerly went along whenever there was a hunt, Felix stayed behind, happy to have the memories of those stags and boars and that one red fox shining in his mind.

By the time they left Poland, Maisie was ready to go home.

"If I have to collect one more berry or dig for one more mushroom," she grumbled to Felix, "I'm going to lose my mind."

"I think it would be nice if we went back to

Livadia," Felix said. He could picture that egg beside the others on the mantel.

Maisie groaned.

"I know you're all friendly with Anastasia, but I'm done here. Let's just give her the egg and go."

"How do you know it goes to Anastasia?" Felix hedged. "There are four Grand Duchesses and one Tsarevich."

"Fine," Maisie said. "Let's try every one of them. Eventually it will land in the right hands."

"But we haven't even seen St. Petersburg yet," Felix said. "Anastasia said that her mother has the most beautiful chambers in the world there."

"Beautiful *chambers*?" Maisie repeated. "I don't care about beautiful chambers. And I also have absolutely no interest in freezing in St. Petersburg."

Felix shuffled his feet and stared down at the floor.

"Is this about that horrid Anastasia?" Maisie asked him. "Is that why you don't want to leave?"

"She isn't horrid," Felix said. "She's wonderful."

"Then *you* stay," Maisie said. "I'm going home."

Felix still didn't look up.

Maisie watched him carefully.

"You did find the egg, didn't you?" she said.

Felix still didn't look up or answer her.

"Didn't you?" she persisted.

"Sort of," he said.

"Either you did or you didn't," Maisie insisted.

"I know where it is," he explained. "But I don't have it."

"Where is it, then?"

"Back at Livadia," he admitted.

"Are they ever going back there?" Maisie asked, panicked. "Do we have to wait until next Easter?"

Felix finally looked up.

"I don't know," he said.

"But that's seven more months!" she cried.

To Felix, seven months with the royal family did not sound terrible. The Grand Duchesses had told him about life at Tsarskoe Selo in St. Petersburg, and it sounded like a never-ending skating and sledding party with a few fancy balls thrown in.

But he could see how upset his sister was, so Felix said, "Anyway, we haven't learned a lesson yet. So even if we did have the egg, and even if we gave it to the right person, we still wouldn't be able to go home."

Maisie glared at him.

"I've learned a lesson," she said.

Before Felix could respond, she continued: "To never time travel with you again!"

That very night, two things happened that made Maisie feel better.

At tea, the Empress appeared with Alexei.

The Tsarevich had dirty-blond hair, gray eyes, and a dimple in each cheek. He was wearing a sailor suit very much like the one Felix wore, and he carried a spaniel named Joy in his arms.

"So you're our guests from America?" he said.

Felix, Maisie, and Alex Andropov nodded.

"I'm the heir to the Russian throne," he said proudly. "And that means you have to stand up when I enter the room."

"Don't be rude," Tatiana scolded gently.

"It's true!" Alexei insisted.

"All right," he said, reluctantly. "You don't have to stand if you don't want to."

He studied each of their faces thoughtfully.

"Do you have a bicycle?" he asked Felix.

"Um . . . yes," Felix answered.

"Do you?" he asked Alex.

Alex shook his head. "I'm not allowed," he said.

Alexei's eyes grew bright.

"Neither am I!" he said. "We should be best friends, then."

"All right," Alex said.

Alexei narrowed his eyes.

"Do you play a lot of tennis?"

"None," Alex said.

Alexei grinned. "Wonderful!"

Just then, Olga burst into the room, her cheeks flushed.

"I have the most lovely news!" she said.

Olga didn't wait for anyone to ask her what her news was. "Mama is giving me a full dress ball for my birthday!" she said happily.

Maria and Tatiana shrieked with delight.

"Olga is turning sixteen in November," Anastasia explained to the others.

"I hope we're still here for it," Maisie said, trying to sound sincere.

Anastasia's eyes widened. "But you must stay for it! You must!"

"What color will you wear?" Maria said dreamily.

"Where will the ball be held?" Tatiana asked.

Olga smiled. "At Livadia," she said. "Isn't that perfect?"

Felix smiled, too. "Yes," he agreed with relief. "Perfect."

❋

In September, they boarded the Imperial train back to Livadia.

The train had blue cars with the gold double-eagle crest on them. To Felix, it was like a palace. Ornate cars for the Tsar and Tsarina included a private study for him; a sitting room for her in her favorite color, mauve; and a huge bathroom with a specially designed bathtub that didn't slosh water, even when the train was moving. The children had their own suite of cars, too, and there were compartments for all the staff. The dining car had a kitchen almost the size of the one at Elm Medona, and a dining-room table that seated twenty people.

As they stepped aboard the train, Maisie grabbed Felix and whispered, "Get that egg."

"I know!" he said, then hurried to catch up to Anastasia.

Alex Andropov appeared beside Maisie, looking pale.

"Are you sick?" she asked him.

"No, it's just . . ."

"What?" she said impatiently.

"Well, I heard the aides-de-camps talking about the threat of a bomb," he said.

"Where?" Maisie asked, dread creeping into her stomach.

"Here," Alex said. "The train. You know the revolutionaries don't like the Tsar."

By now they had reached the children's quarters.

"Maybe we should get off?" Maisie said as she felt the train start to move.

Something caught her eye out the window. "Alex! Look!"

She pointed to another train, also with blue cars and the gold double-eagle crests chugging behind them.

"Do you think the bomb is in there?" Maisie asked, frightened.

But Alex was grinning.

"That's a decoy train," he said. "The revolutionaries won't know which is the right one, so we're probably safe. Clever, eh?"

But Maisie was trembling too much to appreciate

the cleverness of a duplicate decoy train. Instead, she sunk onto one of the white sofas and closed her eyes. *Felix had better find that egg,* she thought. *Fast.*

❄

Maria came into Maisie's room that evening.

"It's time for *zakouski*," she said.

"What's that?" Maisie asked, wearily. She still had not fully recovered from her fright over a possible bomb earlier. And *zakouski* apparently didn't have another translation, so even with the shard, *zakouski* was just *zakouski*.

"You know, little snacks," Maria said. "Come on."

Maisie didn't have much of an appetite, but she followed Maria through the train to the dining car, where everyone was standing around eating from a big buffet of food.

Felix was happily spooning something black onto his plate beside cucumbers and radishes.

When he saw Maisie, he smiled. "Caviar," he said, pointing to the black stuff. "Can you believe it? It's delicious."

What's next? Maisie wondered as she took some slices of ham. Now her brother, the pickiest eater in the world, was eating fish eggs. And liking it.

She took a bite of ham, and then another. Most of the food was fish—sardines and salmon and herring. At least they had some good ham.

Alex Andropov sidled over to her, his plate full of everything the buffet offered.

"I'm surprised you like that," he said, impressed.

Maisie chewed more ham and shrugged.

Alex laughed. "Well, not many Americans like the idea of eating reindeer tongue, that's all."

Maisie stopped chewing.

"Reindeer *tongue?*" she said, spitting what she had in her mouth into her hand.

Alex laughed harder.

"That's disgusting!" Maisie said.

Felix looked over at her.

Maisie mouthed: *Find that egg. Fast.*

❄

The preparations for Olga's birthday ball took up all the time back at Livadia. With so many people in the palace, it was easy for Felix to move around unnoticed. Everyone was more interested in getting fit for their gowns, having their hair cut and curled and pinned, festooning the rooms with decorations, tending the gardens, and dozens of other tasks than noticing what Felix was up to.

Almost immediately upon arriving, he went to the room where the eggs had been displayed on the large marble mantel.

The room had already been transformed for the ball. The chandelier sparkled even more than usual. The floor gleamed with polish. The scent of white roses in enormous crystal vases hung in the air.

Felix paused in the doorway to take in the beauty of the decorations before he began to cross the gleaming floor.

But halfway into the room he stopped and stared.

The eggs were all gone.

In their place sat a large black-and-white photograph of Olga, her hair piled high on her head, and the smallest hint of a smile on her face. The picture had been placed in a gold frame decorated with shiny rubies. It was smack in the center of the mantel, with vases of white roses on either side of it, and not one Fabergé egg anywhere in sight.

As if he were seeing a mirage, Felix went over to the mantel just to be sure.

He stood, staring up into Olga's face, his heart sinking.

How could he tell Maisie that the egg was gone?

❄

Maisie was certain that Felix was avoiding her. Caught up in the excitement of the ball, he'd probably forgotten to retrieve the egg. She had to admit that the excitement was contagious—Maisie was looking forward to the ball, too. She'd even wrapped the invitation in tissue paper to preserve it, tracing the scrolls and curlicues of the letters. Even though they'd written her name as Maisie Pickworth, Maisie still loved the way the invitation looked and read:

Their Imperial Majesties invite you to dinner and a dancing party to be held on Thursday November 3rd, 1911, at 6:45 in the evening, at the Livadia Palace

Maisie Pickworth

Military cavaliers in frock coat with epaulets.

Civilians in evening dress with white tie.

Still, she wanted to be home and sit on her pink pouf and eat potato chips with James Ferocious beside her.

For Olga's birthday, her parents gave her a

diamond ring and necklace with more pearls and diamonds than Maisie could count. All the Grand Duchesses wore white gowns, except for Olga. Hers was pink, and with the sparkling necklace and her hair swept up in curls, she looked lovelier than anyone Maisie had ever seen.

Before the ball began, dinner was served with everyone seated at small round tables set with heavy ornate silver, flickering white candles, and flowers from the Empress's garden at Livadia. The Tsar and his wife sat the head table with Grand Dukes and Duchesses and ministers of this and that. Maisie, stuck at a table with a bunch of kids, including the Prince of Greece, who ate with his mouth open and whined all during dinner, couldn't stop watching Olga and her table. Olga's cheeks were pink from excitement, and she kept whispering to her escort, a dark-haired handsome boy with intense brown eyes. Tatiana was at that table, too, and so was the Emir of Bukhara, whatever that was. It all looked much more interesting than the kids' table, that was for sure. Of course Felix got to sit with Anastasia and Maria at a table where everyone seemed to be having much more fun than Maisie.

"I don't like beets," the Prince of Greece whined.

"Then don't eat them," Maisie grumbled.

The Crimean regimental band began playing loud music, as if they were at a parade. At least she wouldn't have to listen to the Prince of Greece anymore, Maisie decided, eyeing Olga as she beamed at her escort.

Finally, dinner ended. But that only began the endless presentations of the guests to the Tsar and his wife. Maisie thought they would never end. But of course they did, and when she returned to the dining room, all the tables were gone and the whole room had been transformed for dancing. Still more flowers filled the room, and an orchestra began to play a waltz as soon as the guests walked in. In a flash, couples waltzed past Maisie and Alex Andropov, who stood awkwardly, afraid they'd be forced to dance, too. But no one even noticed them.

Alex elbowed Maisie lightly.

"Look at the Empress," he whispered, indicating across the room where the Empress sat in an armchair beside a column with Alexei, who was dressed in a white sailor suit and watching the party. She looked miserable.

"Why doesn't she join in?" Maisie asked Alex.

"She doesn't like parties," Alex explained with a shrug.

It was clear even from where they stood that the Tsarevich wanted to stay at the party, his eyes shining as he watched the dancers and the musicians. But the Empress was urging him to leave with her.

The orchestra began a lively song.

"The mazurka!" Alex said, clapping his hands in time.

Maisie saw the Tsar march over to his son, lift him up, and carry him out, the Empress right behind them.

That poor kid never gets to have any fun, Maisie thought. But she kept it to herself.

The Grand Duchesses floated past on the arms of handsome soldiers. Except Anastasia, of course. She was doing the mazurka with Felix. He didn't even notice Maisie as he twirled past her.

At some point, the glass doors were opened onto the rose gardens, and the entire palace smelled floral and sweet.

"I never want to leave," Alex whispered, his eyes moist.

"Not you, too," Maisie moaned.

Alex tipped his chin in the direction of Felix,

who stood across the room beside a giggling Anastasia.

"I'm guessing you're referring to your bewitched brother," Alex said.

Maisie nodded.

"I haven't asked you yet," Alex began, then stopped himself.

"Let's step outside," he said. "I don't want anyone to overhear us."

Maisie followed him into the gardens, the scent of roses even heavier there. A full moon hung in the starry sky.

"What do you want to ask me?" Maisie said to Alex.

"How do you get back?" he asked her.

"I don't really know how it works," Maisie admitted. "But we need an object to travel in the first place—"

"The Fabergé egg?"

"That's how we got here, yes."

Maisie told him about all the other objects—the letter for Clara Barton, the coin for Alexander Hamilton, the jade box of dirt for Pearl Buck, the handcuffs for Harry Houdini, the feather for Crazy

Horse, the crown for Queen Liliuokalani, the device for Alexander Graham Bell, the flight instrument for Amelia Earhart, the Florentine seal for Leonardo da Vinci.

"They have to give us something, too," Maisie explained. "But not an object."

"What then?"

"Advice. Kind of a lesson that will help us in our real lives."

"So if a person wanted to stay," Alex said slowly, "he would have to get rid of the object."

"Alex! No!" Maisie blurted.

She thought about Great-Aunt Maisie staying with Harry Houdini and what that meant in the present.

"But it would be impossible to avoid hearing advice," Alex continued, talking more to himself than to Maisie. He nodded. "Yes, the only way to stay is to destroy the object," he said matter-of-factly.

"You can't do that, Alex," Maisie pleaded. "Then none of us would get home, and that's not fair."

In the light of the full moon, Maisie could see his eyes clearly. And in them she saw the glint of determination, of a mind made up.

"Of course," Alex said, starting back toward the house, "nothing can be done until we get to Tsarskoe Selo."

Maisie grabbed his arm, hard.

"What do you mean?"

"That's where it is," he said, trying unsuccessfully to wiggle free of her grasp.

"Where *what* is?" Maisie insisted.

Alex lifted his chin defiantly and didn't reply.

"The egg?" Maisie realized. "The egg isn't here?"

He shook his head.

"All of them were packed up and sent to St. Petersburg," he said, finally getting free of her.

"You're lying," Maisie said, hoping that he was indeed not telling her the truth.

"Ask any one of the royal family," Alex said. "They'll tell you the eggs are all at the palace there. Unlike you, I thought to ask them."

"Oh no," Maisie moaned.

"I'm sorry," Alex said softly. "But as soon as we get to Tsarskoe Selo, I'm destroying that egg."

"Please—" she began.

But Alex cut her off.

"I belong here," he said. "And I'm not going back."

CHAPTER NINE

TSARSKOE SELO

Felix was in the middle of the most wonderful dream about swimming in the Black Sea with Anastasia when he got roughly shaken awake. It took him a minute to realize he wasn't in the sea at all, but instead was in bed with Maisie staring at him with a panicked look on her face.

"What's wrong?" Felix asked.

"Alex Andropov, that's what's wrong," Maisie said.

And she began to cry.

"What did he do?" Felix said, putting his arm around his sister's shoulders.

"It's what he's *about* to do," Maisie said through her tears.

"Maisie, you're talking in riddles. Tell me."

Maisie wiped her eyes and cheeks, and sniffled.

"He doesn't want to go home," she began.

Felix looked away from her. He didn't want her to see that *he* wasn't ready to leave, either.

"So he asked me how we get back, and when I told him, he said he was going to destroy the Fabergé egg before we could give it to whomever we're supposed to give it to," Maisie said, her words coming out in a rush.

Then she burst into tears again.

"Don't worry," Felix told her. "I looked for the egg when we got here and it had been moved. They all had. Probably to decorate for the party. But I'll ask Anastasia where it is and—"

"It's not here!" Maisie said through a fresh round of tears.

"I'm sure it is," Felix said, although he wasn't sure at all.

Maisie shook her head adamantly.

"They've packed up all the eggs and sent them to St. Petersburg."

"Why would they do that?" Felix wondered out loud.

"I don't know," Maisie said, "but they did. And Alex threatened to find it as soon as we arrive at Tsarskoe Selo and to destroy it, and then we'll never be able to leave!"

Felix gulped. As much as he wanted to stay longer, the thought of not being able to leave at all, of never seeing his parents again, of facing the Bolsheviks . . . It was all too much for him, and he burst into tears, too.

"You can't cry!" Maisie told him. "You need to help me figure out how to stop Alex Andropov!"

But Felix had no idea how they were going to do that.

It took two days to get to St. Petersburg by the Imperial train, a mostly boring journey past lots of nothing—no villages or farms or people, just endless Russia. Felix purposely sat next to Alex as the train bumped slowly along, which made Anastasia furious. But Felix could not think of how to find the egg before Alex did, and his only hope was to try to talk him out of destroying it.

"You can save your breath," Alex said as soon as Felix sat down. He was reading a fat novel in Russian and didn't even bother to look up.

"Alex," Felix began, anyway, "I know it seems like a good idea to stay, but your life here isn't going to be any better than at home. Think about it."

Alex turned the page.

"I have," he said. "My mind's made up."

"But what about your . . . your sickness," Felix said cautiously.

Although Alex still stared down at the book, Felix could tell he had his attention.

"We're in 1911," Felix continued. "I'm pretty sure they've made a lot of progress with treating hemophilia in a century. If you should get sick here—"

"Actually," Alex said, "they haven't made very much progress."

"But modern hospitals can take better care of you," Felix insisted. "Conditions in 1911—"

Alex sighed. "Forget it, Felix," he said, returning his full attention to Tolstoy.

As they approached the Imperial park near St. Petersburg in a series of Imperial carriages, Felix finally realized how to keep the egg safe from Alex Andropov. He had an ally besides Maisie: Anastasia. Surely she would help him keep the egg safe. The park was bordered by an iron fence and guarded by men on horseback dressed in bright red uniforms and tall fur hats, with swords at their sides. Anastasia had been cold toward Felix ever since he sat with Alex on the train, but suddenly she appeared next to him, pointing as they entered the gates and moved toward Tsarskoe Selo.

The snow-covered ground twinkled under the gray sky.

"That's the Turkish bath," Anastasia announced as they passed a pale pink building.

When Felix saw a Chinese pagoda set among tall snow-laden trees, he said, "Wow! Look at that!"

Anastasia smiled at him. "I knew you would love it here," she said happily.

"You're not mad at me anymore?" Felix asked hopefully.

"Well," Anastasia admitted, "a little."

Felix knew it was time to put his plan in motion.

"I had to talk to Alex," he said, his voice low. "I know that he's your cousin, but . . . well . . ."

Anastasia looked worried.

"My sister gave your mother an egg," Felix began. "A Fabergé egg?"

"Yes," Anastasia said. "With a peacock inside."

"For some reason," Felix said, "Alex wants to destroy it."

"Destroy one of Carl Fabergé's masterpieces?" Anastasia said, covering her mouth in shock. "But why?"

This was the moment Felix was dreading, even when he'd hatched the plan. He was not a good liar, and he didn't like to do it. But he couldn't risk having Alex find the egg first.

"I think he's jealous," Felix said.

"Of what?"

"Of your family," Felix said, his throat dry. "He doesn't usually live in such grand surroundings, and I don't think he can help himself from getting a little jealous."

Anastasia considered this.

Then she nodded slowly. "I can understand that, I think," she said. "There are people . . ." She paused, swallowing hard. "People who say terrible things about Papa, and maybe Alex has been influenced by such talk."

"I don't know about that," Felix said, nervously. "But I do know what he's planning to do when we arrive at the Alexander Palace."

Anastasia and Felix stared out the window of the coach just as the Alexander Palace came into view.

Before they'd left Livadia, the Tsar had explained to Maisie, Felix, and Alex how Catherine I, back in 1717, had wanted a country retreat from St. Petersburg. Tsarskoe Selo, only fifteen miles away, was chosen as the location for the new palace. Catherine's daughter Elizabeth tore down the original palace and built a new one to rival Versailles in France. But the Tsar and his family chose to live in the smaller one that Catherine had built for her grandson, the Tsar's father, Alexander III.

Felix had imagined that the smaller palace, called the Alexander Palace, would resemble Elm Medona. But he saw that it was only small in comparison to the Catherine Palace that stood beside it. The Catherine Palace was an enormous blue-and-white building.

"Over two hundred rooms," Anastasia told Felix when she saw him gaping at it. "Have you heard of the Amber Room?"

Felix shook his head.

"Oh, you must see it! I'll take you over. It has

amber mosaics and amber panels and . . . well, it's just beautiful! Over four hundred and fifty kilograms of amber!" she explained.

"Whoa!" he said, happy that he'd gotten an A on that conversion test last week. "That's half a ton!"

The carriage was slowing now at the entrance to the Alexander Palace.

"Wait until you see Mama's boudoir," Anastasia said proudly. "It's the most beautiful room in all of Russia. Maybe in all of the world!"

"Anastasia?" Felix asked.

She turned to look at him.

"You'll get to that egg first, won't you?"

"Of course!" she said. "I know exactly where all of the Fabergé eggs are kept, and I'll take the one from you and Maisie and hide it."

Felix chewed his bottom lip, thinking.

In front of them swarmed more soldiers than he'd ever seen in one place, dressed in many different kinds of uniforms.

"Maybe you could give it to me," Felix suggested. "Alex would never think that I'd have it."

"Good idea!" Anastasia said, cheerfully. Then, her face grew serious. "Poor Alex! We'll have to make him feel special, won't we?"

"Yes," Felix said, his relief so great that he found himself grinning from ear to ear. "Let's do that."

Maisie could remember in great detail that hot, humid day last summer when she, Felix, and their mother had arrived at Elm Medona. She remembered how cranky and sad she'd felt, and also how enormous Elm Medona had seemed to her then. Standing in front of the Catherine and Alexander Palaces, Maisie almost laughed at the memory. These things weren't enormous, they were gigantic!

Or . . .

She tried to think of other synonyms for *enormous*.

Colossal!

Mammoth!

Epic!

Felix would appreciate her synonyms, Maisie thought, if he weren't mooning over Anastasia.

Maisie sighed. Now that she couldn't trust Alex, she felt alone again and left out.

Even when Maria came over to her and linked her arm in Maisie's, Maisie didn't feel much better.

"Get ready for life here in Tsarskoe Selo," Maria said.

"What does that mean?" Maisie asked.

Not only wasn't she ready for life here, she was ready to go home.

"You'll see," Maria said.

To Maisie, it sounded like some kind of a warning.

Life at Tsarskoe Selo was so regimented that Maisie thought she might lose her mind. The days at Livadia and aboard the *Standart* had a sameness to them that Maisie found boring. But the days at Tsarskoe Selo made her feel like she was in the army.

"It's protocol," Olga had explained. "It's been the same for hundreds of years."

At first the dazzling uniforms the servants wore impressed Maisie. Scarlet capes and ostrich-plumed hats, the Imperial double-headed eagle emblazoned everywhere. But the way the servants had to bow when anyone in the royal family—even Alexei— entered a room; the way no one—not even Maisie or Felix or Alex Andropov—could speak to anyone in the royal family until they were spoken to; the way the Tsar made people lower their eyes, pay attention to him, remain quiet around him—it all made Maisie uncomfortable. When other noble people who lived in the mansions in the town of Tsarskoe Selo were invited for tea or an audience with the Tsar, they acted so excited that Maisie almost felt embarrassed for them.

The Alexander Palace was designed with a central area for official meetings, a wing off that for the servants' quarters, and another wing for the family.

It was life here that Maisie found so interminable, the routine so rigid that she understood why Anastasia acted naughty.

The Tsar insisted his daughters get up at seven and have breakfast with him. But seven in St. Petersburg during the winter meant it was still dark out. And cold. Empress Alexandra didn't get out of bed until the afternoon, simply moving from the bedroom to her private boudoir, the one the Duchesses told Maisie and Felix was considered the most beautiful room in Russia.

The Duchesses went there after breakfast so that their mother could choose their clothes for the day. When they left to be examined—every morning!— by the court physician, the Empress lolled around in her flowy dresses, writing letters, and playing with her hateful dog, Eira. Maisie peeked into the boudoir and saw for herself the mauve walls, carpets, and furniture. Even the flowers were purple—roses, lilacs, violets. It seemed unfair to Maisie that her own mother worked hours and hours every day at Fishbaum and Fishbaum, dressed in her wrinkled suits and kitten heels. But wasn't that what made her mother so interesting? The Empress always had a melancholy look on her face. Maybe, Maisie decided, she was just bored, even though she was helping to run an empire.

Meanwhile, the Grand Duchesses started their lessons every day at nine on the dot. Although they got to go outside and play in the snow for an hour before lunch, all afternoon they were stuck inside with a series of tutors, moving from one lesson to the next without pause.

Maisie and Felix didn't see them all day, except for at lunch, which was so formal that Maisie was afraid to do something wrong. The Imperial priest, dressed completely in black except for the giant silver cross that hung around his neck, and with a beard that seemed to never end, rang a bell to begin the meal. The Empress never joined them, preferring to stay in her boudoir with Alexei. Maisie figured out that she probably wanted to protect him from getting injured and having an episode, but still it seemed odd that she kept so much to herself. In the afternoon, she went out in her carriage, surrounded by footmen and coachmen, while the Tsar rode his horse through the surrounding villages.

Then, at exactly 4:00 PM everyone gathered for tea. The Tsar always had two glasses and one piece of bread with butter. There was never anything sweet like cake or cookies at tea. Just bread and butter. But the Grand Duchesses loved that part of the day. They even changed their clothes just for tea, and sat together knitting or embroidering.

"I think I might lose my mind," Maisie whispered to Felix as she watched the Tsar refuse a third cup of tea. Just once, she wished he'd do something different.

"Well," Felix said with a smile, "I have something exciting to show you."

"You do?" Maisie said.

"Follow me."

Maisie followed Felix through the endless series

of drawing rooms and anterooms, to the door that led from the family's quarters to the central part of the palace.

There, four large Ethiopian bodyguards patrolled in bright red pants and shiny gold jackets. They wore shoes that looked like Aladdin's with their curled toes, and white turbans wrapped around their heads.

"Maisie," Felix said, "meet Jim Hercules."

To Maisie's surprise, Jim Hercules said, "Pleased to meet you," in an American accent.

"What?" Maisie said. "You're *American*?"

"From Alabama," Jim Hercules said.

"But why are you here? Dressed like that?"

Jim Hercules's face grew serious.

"My parents were slaves," he said softly. "And I fled the United States for London to escape the bigotry there. I feel at home here," he added.

"Do you ever get to go back to America?" Maisie asked, her own homesickness giving her an ache.

He nodded. "Every year," he said.

"Jim Hercules has helped us," Felix told Maisie.

"He has?"

"I've hidden the egg from Alex," Jim Hercules said proudly.

"But *we* can get to it, can't we?" Maisie asked, afraid he'd hidden it too well.

"Oh yes," Jim Hercules said. "Whenever you want to."

CHAPTER TEN

THE HOLY MAN

"What we need to do," Maisie explained to Felix, trying to sound patient, "is give the egg to Anastasia. Then, in case we've had a lesson and not even realized it, we'll go right home."

The very idea made her smile. Last summer, she would never have believed that Elm Medona would feel like home, or that she'd want to go back there more than anywhere else, even 10 Bethune Street.

"But if we haven't had a lesson and we give Anastasia the egg and Alex sees it, we're doomed," Felix said, stalling what was surely the inevitable: going home.

Maisie would have argued with him, but Anastasia came into the drawing room and said with great excitement, "We're going sledding! Come on!"

It had been snowing for days, and just this morning when the sun finally came up at nine, it illuminated a snow-covered landscape with icicles glistening from trees.

Felix rushed out, happy to end *that* conversation.

He heard Maisie asking, "Will Alexei come, too?"

"Oh no," came Tatiana's voice, "he'll stay in his room and play with his trains."

His entire room was filled with mechanical toys: ships and trains and factories, soldiers and workmen and townsfolk, all of it sent into motion by the Tsarevich with a flip of a switch.

"But Alexander Andropov will join us," Tatiana added.

"Great," Maisie said, hoping Tatiana couldn't detect that she felt just the opposite.

The four Grand Duchesses were wrapped in white fur coats with matching hats and muffs, as was Maisie. They sat on the wooden sleds, and raced down the snowy hills laughing with delight. Even Maisie had to admit that this snow-covered landscape looked magical, like something from a fairy tale.

And the air, though very cold, felt crisp and fresh, like the purest winter air ever.

Felix raced Anastasia, their cheeks bright red.

Alex sidled up to Maisie.

"I'll find it," he said, "no matter where you hid it."

Rather than answer him, Maisie jumped on her sled and flew down the snowy hill. She loved the wind in her face, and the way she heard only it and nothing else.

Until a scream pierced the air.

Maisie brought her sled to a swooshing stop and stood, looking for whom that scream belonged to.

Alex Andropov lay in a heap at the bottom of the hill.

Serves him right, Maisie thought.

But Felix looked terrified.

Then, in the quiet, Maisie heard Felix telling the Grand Duchesses what she had forgotten:

"We have to get a doctor!" Felix said, panicked. "He has hemophilia."

The Empress Alexandra, who had been an elusive and mysterious presence all these months, appeared suddenly at Alex Andropov's bedside. She was beautiful in her loose white dress and fair skin, her auburn hair held in soft curls gathered with a diamond barrette that sparkled in the lamplight like the snow outside.

She rested a hand on Alex's forehead.

"Where does it hurt, darling?" she asked, her German accent so different than the Russian ones Maisie and Felix had grown used to hearing.

Alex's face twisted with pain.

"Ankle," he managed to say.

The Empress folded down the white bedsheet to reveal his twisted, bruised, and swollen left ankle.

She nodded grimly, and tears wet her cheeks.

"Prepare a mud bath," she ordered one servant.

To another she said, "Bring one of the Tsarevich's devices, please."

Gently, she pulled the sheet around Alex.

"I'll be back soon," she said. "Rest."

"Mud bath?" Felix said, anxiously, after she left the room. "You need more than a mud bath, Alex!"

Alex squeezed his eyes shut, either from pain or to ignore Felix, or both.

"What would they do at home?" Maisie asked.

"Maybe we can do that here."

Alex shook his head.

Now Felix saw tears on his cheeks, too.

"Plasma," Alex said, writhing with pain.

Felix looked to Maisie for help understanding.

"You mean a transfusion?" she asked Alex, who simply nodded.

"Do they know about transfusions yet?" Felix wondered aloud.

Again Alex shook his head.

"There's nothing else?" Felix asked desperately.

As mad as he was at Alex, he couldn't bear to see someone in so much pain. In fact, he was certain he'd never seen anyone suffer like this. And it seemed to be getting worse.

"I suspect," Alex panted, "that this device they're bringing . . ." He groaned again. "It's probably a heavy iron one," he said.

"Will that help at all?" Felix said hopefully.

Alex shrugged. "Will hurt," he said. "Mine is made of plastic."

Maisie winced.

"Maybe I could massage your ankle?" Felix offered. Once, when he'd sprained his ankle, his father had put ice on it to reduce the swelling and massaged it carefully.

"No!" Alex said, half-sitting. "That can cause a new hemorrhage!"

A loud clatter at the door caused Maisie and Felix to turn their attention away from Alex to see what had arrived.

Two servants wheeled in what must have been the iron device the Empress had ordered. It looked more like an instrument of torture than a healing instrument.

"Go," Alex whispered, his feverish eyes also focused on the iron contraption. "Please."

Maisie and Felix did not hesitate. They hurried out of the room, gripping each other.

Alex Andropov's screams could be heard all the way in the room where everyone gathered for the usual four o'clock tea.

"Isn't there medicine for the pain?" Felix asked.

"Morphine," Maria said.

"But Mama and Papa don't believe in using it," Tatiana added.

"Why not?" Maisie asked in disbelief. "I mean, listen to him."

"It's addictive," Olga explained. "If they gave it to Alexei every time he had an episode . . ."

She didn't have to finish the sentence. Her meaning was clear. By now, the little boy would be addicted to morphine.

Maisie couldn't even eat her bread and butter, though the Tsar seemed unaware of the screams coming from Alex's room. He sat going over his papers and news dispatches, sipping his second glass of tea.

"Can't you do something?" Maisie asked him angrily.

The Tsar looked at her wearily.

"If I could fix him," he said quietly, "wouldn't I have fixed my own son by now?"

"But he's in such pain!" Maisie said.

"With luck," the Tsar said, "he will get through this alive."

"You mean," Felix stammered, "he might die?"

"That is always the risk," the Tsar said, sadly.

A servant offered him another glass of tea, but as usual he refused. Instead, he stood and asked for his horse to be prepared.

The Grand Duchesses returned to their lessons.

And Maisie and Felix went back outside into the

cold, darkening St. Petersburg afternoon to avoid the screams of pain coming from Alexander Andropov.

The next morning, the Empress appeared at breakfast.

So unusual was this sight that the Grand Duchesses jumped to their feet, dropping their napkins to the floor and covering their mouths with their hands.

"Sunny!" the Tsar blurted, also standing abruptly and using his special nickname for her.

"The boy," she said. "He's much worse."

"Worse?" Maisie asked, unable to imagine that anyone could suffer still more.

The Empress took the Tsar's hands in hers.

"I've called for the Holy Man," she said simply.

Anastasia touched Felix's shoulder.

"He will save Alex's life," she whispered. "You'll see."

Even though Felix wanted Alex to recover, he wasn't at all confident that a priest was the person to save Alex's life.

The entire household, including the Empress and

Alexei, gathered that evening to greet this Holy Man when he arrived.

To Felix's surprise, Anastasia called, "He's here!" with great excitement as a dirty man with long matted hair and an even more unkempt beard got out of a coach and walked toward the entrance of the Alexander Palace.

"That's the man who's going to save Alex?" Maisie blurted.

"Yes," Tatiana said reverentially.

As the man neared, Felix saw that his wrinkled face had deep pockmarks.

The man removed his long, black threadbare coat and deposited it gruffly in the hands of one of the footmen. Beneath the coat he wore obviously fine, expensive clothes: a canary-yellow silk shirt covered with embroidered birds and flowers in every color of the rainbow, tight black velvet pants with knee-high leather boots, and a pale blue silk cord around his waist with huge tassels hanging from it.

Felix's eyes focused on the large gold cross around the man's neck.

But Maisie was almost immediately transfixed by the man's eyes.

They were the color of steel, a light gray that seemed both translucent and impenetrable at the same time.

And the man had set his gaze on Maisie.

He ignored all the others with their outstretched arms and words of greeting, and walked over directly to Maisie.

"Who are you?" he asked.

Before Maisie could answer, he continued questioning her.

"Why are you here in St. Petersburg? Are your parents with you? Are you happy?"

This last question caught her so off guard that Maisie burst into tears.

The man wrapped his arms around her, and his strong stench of body odor and filth enveloped her. Yet she didn't mind, somehow.

"Your parents have disappointed you," he said firmly. "Everyone has disappointed you."

"Yes!" Maisie said, sobbing now.

"Let go of all that disappointment, or you will never move forward," he said.

He released Maisie from his arms and went to each person in turn, taking their hands and looking directly into their eyes, holding their gaze for a long moment before going to the next person.

Anastasia whispered, "Is it true?"

"Yes," Maisie managed to whisper.

"Yes," Felix agreed.

"But your family is everything," Anastasia told them. "You must remember that."

"It is necessary to have faith," the Holy Man said, his stinking breath coming out in puffs of cold air.

Finally, he turned his attention to the Empress.

"Mother," he said to her, and that mesmerizing stare focused on the Empress, whose knees buckled slightly under its intensity.

Maisie couldn't believe that this man could call the Empress *Mother*, that he spoke without being spoken to, that rather than bow or step back from her, he boldly walked right up to her.

"Gregory," the Empress said in a shaky voice.

"Bring me to the boy," he said, and strode into the palace, the royal family skittering after *him*.

In Alex's dark bedroom, everyone stood around the bed, leaving room for the Holy Man to stand close to Alex. Candles flickered, sending shadows dancing across the faces of those gathered there.

The Holy Man spoke in low hypnotic tones, his large dirty hands resting on Alex's forehead.

"In Pokrovskoe, on the Tura River, in western Siberia," he intoned, "there is great freedom. It is there that I, burning with fever in my bed, a mere boy of twelve like you and your friends here, sat up and pointed a finger at the horse thief everyone was searching for."

Felix blinked. How did this man know that they were twelve years old?

Gregory continued, telling stories of Siberia and nature and faith.

His voice seemed to soothe the people and even the room itself.

After a very long time, Alex Andropov opened his eyes.

Gregory locked his on Alex's.

Felix found himself holding his breath.

Until, suddenly, the Holy Man turned to face the others.

"The boy will live," he said simply.

At that, the Empress let out a sob of relief and took those dirty hands in her pure white ones, kissing each with gratitude.

"Do not let the doctors near him," he said.

"Whatever you ask," the Empress said.

The Holy Man smiled, revealing stained crooked teeth.

"I wonder, Mother," he said, "if my favorite fish soup is waiting for me."

"Of course, of course," she said.

Again, the Holy Man walked ahead of the royal family. Again, they followed him.

But Maisie and Felix stayed behind with Alex.

"Are you all right?" Maisie asked dubiously.

Alex nodded weakly.

He said something, his voice hoarse and soft.

"What?" Felix said, leaning closer.

"Rasputin," Alex whispered.

CHAPTER ELEVEN

A SURPRISE GUEST

That night by Alexander Andropov's bedside, Rasputin showed them his healing powers. But Maisie and Felix didn't really understand them until Alex got strong enough to come down to breakfast again several days later.

Outside the all-white dining room, the winter sky was still dark. A servant had parted the heavy blue-and-silver curtains so that the first rays of sunlight would come in. A porcelain stove made of vivid ornate tiles kept the room warm and cozy. Periodically, a footman walked through the room with a swinging pot of smoldering incense, leaving behind a trail of sandalwood smoke.

When the Tsar left to go into his office and the

Grand Duchesses began their lessons, Alex, still pale and weak, said: "Rasputin healed me. If only I could tell Babushka."

"I thought his name was Gregory," Felix said.

Alex nodded. "Gregory Efimovich," he said. "But when he was a young boy he was given this nickname of Rasputin."

"What does it mean?" Maisie asked.

"Dissolute," Alex said.

"Okay," Maisie said, "and what does *dissolute* mean?"

Felix answered, "Doesn't it describe someone who's immoral?"

"Yes," Alex told them. "People believe that it's a sign of his humility that he kept such a name."

"Is that why he doesn't take a bath, too?" Maisie said, wrinkling her nose at the memory of Rasputin's pungent body odor.

"He's a mystic, a holy man," Alex explained. "Taking a bath isn't important to him."

"Well," Maisie said firmly, "it should be."

"But why does he dress so fancy, then?" Felix wondered out loud.

"The Empress embroiders his shirts by hand,"

Alex said. "Out of gratitude for saving Alexei's life."

"I think he saved your life, too," Felix said softly.

"But how?" Maisie asked.

"He heals through prayer," Alex said. "In 1907, Alexei had a terrible injury. The doctors tried everything, but ultimately announced that he was going to die. The Tsarina called Rasputin here, to the Alexander Palace, and he healed Alexei. Some people believe he does it through hypnosis. Others believe he is using drugs to save Alexei. But you saw what happened to me, didn't you?"

Remembering Rasputin's eyes holding her gaze, Maisie shuddered.

"I think he's kind of creepy," she said.

"I owe him my life," Alex reminded her.

"But this is proof of what we talked about on the train," Felix said. "When you're back at home, you won't need mud baths or painful iron contraptions or mystics. You'll get a transfusion and you'll get better."

Alex's eyes blazed.

"I'm not going home!" he said angrily.

Maisie said in a quiet voice, "Alex, we are in 1911 St. Petersburg. In seven years the entire royal family is going to be massacred. You have to leave. Now."

"Aha!" Alex said. "I've thought of that. But since I know that the Tsar will abdicate in February of 1917, and the family will be placed under house arrest then, all I have to do is leave Russia before that happens."

"But where will you go?" Maisie asked. "And what if you *can't* leave?"

Alex shrugged. "I have a long time to work that all out," he said.

The silvery light of morning came through the windows. The wood in the stove crackled.

A footman appeared with more incense, walking across the room and then around its periphery, swinging the gold pot.

As he left, another footman entered with a tall dark-haired woman.

"Madame Brissac," the footman announced.

Madame Brissac smiled a toothy smile.

"You must be Maisie," she said, her eyes examining Maisie coolly. "I've come from St. Petersburg to prepare all the ladies. The Empress has requested I make a gown for you as well, for the ball Friday night."

"All right," Maisie said.

"Stand," Madame Brissac ordered, and Maisie stood.

Madame Brissac walked around Maisie several times, taking notes with a gold pen in a small leather-bound notebook. Periodically, she clicked her tongue against the roof of her mouth, which Maisie took for some kind of disapproval.

Finally, Madame Brissac said, "Fine. I'll call for you later today for a fitting."

She frowned at Maisie.

"What a shame, though," she said, shaking her head. "I can make you one of the most beautiful dresses in all of Russia, but I cannot do anything with that hair."

With that, she walked out.

"I don't even want her to make me a dress," Maisie grumbled, insulted.

"A ball!" Felix said, imagining another dance with Anastasia. "I wonder what the occasion is this time."

"Some special guest from America," Alex said.

"I can't wait until Friday," Felix said dreamily, ignoring Maisie's scowl.

"Meanwhile," Alex said, "I need to find where you've hidden the egg."

"You'll never find it," Felix said.

"Just watch me," Alex said.

Indeed, over the next few days before the ball, Maisie and Felix spotted Alexander Andropov coming in and out of anterooms and drawing rooms, looking inside Chinese vases and porcelain bowls, peeking under tables and behind curtains. Despite his determination, they both knew the egg was safe with Jim Hercules.

Although Maisie did not like Madame Brissac, the white gown with silver threads that she created for Maisie was so beautiful that Maisie threw her arms around the unsuspecting woman.

"Please, please," Madame Brissac sputtered as she disengaged from Maisie's exuberant hug.

Madame Brissac smoothed her own dress and patted her hair.

"Now, you see," she said, "I could not agree to make you a beautiful dress and then have you wear it with that unruly, unmanageable—"

Maisie's cheeks burned red. "So you said," she huffed.

"Yes, yes, well. I arranged for this to be sent from my couturier shop," Madame Brissac said, pulling a small gold box from one of the many pockets in the apron she wore.

The apron was filled with a seemingly endless supply of pins and needles and threads of every color and tiny jeweled scissors and measuring tape.

Maisie took the box, suspicious.

"Well, open it," Madame Brissac said, wearily.

Slowly, Maisie untied the gold ribbon and lifted the lid of the gold box.

Inside, a large barrette sparkled with hundreds of small diamonds.

Maisie gasped.

"So you will lift your hair like this," Madame Brissac instructed, demonstrating in the air between them. "And twist it like so. And then clip it with this. And voilà! Your hair will complement my dress."

"It's so sparkly," Maisie said.

"Yes," Madame Brissac said, collecting her things.

She took off the apron and folded it into her giant bag.

"Thank you," Maisie remembered to say as Madame Brissac walked out.

Maisie went to the triple mirror, still in her

beautiful white-and-silver dress and white suede slippers.

"Lift like this," Maisie said, lifting her tangle of curls.

"Twist like so," she said, awkwardly twisting her hair as Madame Brissac had demonstrated.

"Clip with this," she said, fastening the diamond clip in her hair.

"And voilà!" Maisie ended, her voice full of awe.

Because looking back at her from all three mirrors was a girl who was almost pretty.

To Maisie and Felix's surprise, the ball was not going to be held at the Alexander Palace. Rather, the entire family was going to the Winter Palace in St. Petersburg, fifteen miles away.

Maisie knew that if she asked Felix to get the egg from Jim Hercules, he would refuse. He would argue that if they took it from its hiding place, they risked having Alexander Andropov find it and destroy it. Although that was true, Maisie also believed it was an excuse to stay even longer with Anastasia.

She and Felix had not discussed it, but Maisie also believed that they had received their lesson the night Rasputin arrived: *Your family is everything.*

That's what Anastasia had told them. All they had to do now was give her the Fabergé egg, and they would be back in Elm Medona with their mother, and their father would be nearby.

Your family is everything.

Maisie smiled to herself.

Then she went to find Jim Hercules.

❄

"Mama hates St. Petersburg," Anastasia confided to Felix in the carriage en route to the Winter Palace.

"Why?" Felix asked.

Outside, snow fell so hard that he couldn't see the carriages behind or in front of them.

"She says it's a rotten town and isn't even one atom Russian," Anastasia said. "Even Papa calls it 'the bog.'"

"Then why are they having this ball there?" Felix wondered.

"It's complicated," Anastasia said, thoughtfully. "To Russians, the Winter Palace is the symbol of the power of the Tsar. It has fifteen hundred rooms, almost two thousand windows, and one hundred and seventeen staircases."

"Wow!" Felix said.

"But lately . . ."

Anastasia hesitated, looking sad.

"What is it?" Felix asked, touching her hand.

Anastasia took a deep breath. "Lately, as one of the Grand Dukes told Papa, 'A new and hostile Russia glares through the window as we dance.'"

"Is Russia already hostile toward your family?" Felix asked.

"Already?" Anastasia repeated, surprised.

"I meant . . . just . . . Who's hostile?"

She studied his face carefully.

"Well," she said, finally, "just six years ago something terrible happened there, at the Winter Palace. Papa believes it could be the beginning of more terrible things."

"Was it the Bolsheviks?" Felix asked, a chill spreading up his arms.

"What are they?" Anastasia asked, confused.

"Oh," Felix said, quickly. "Nothing. I'm mixed up, that's all."

"It wasn't these . . . Bolsheviks. No. Father Gapon, a priest that the workers liked very much, brought a hundred thousand of them to protest at the Winter Palace. He had a petition he wanted

Papa to sign, but of course we don't live there. Papa was in Tsarskoe Selo. He didn't even know about the protest! As the demonstrators neared, the Imperial troops fired on them—"

"Oh no!" Felix said. "People were killed?"

Anastasia nodded solemnly.

"Everyone calls it Bloody Sunday now," she added with a shiver.

"Bloody Sunday," Felix repeated softly.

"That began a revolution. Not just workers, but farmers and peasants. Even students!

"Papa told us that reports estimated two million workers went on strike that fall."

Anastasia smiled at Felix.

"Don't look so glum, Felix! Papa fixed everything. He signed a new constitution and did all sorts of things to make people happy again."

Felix looked away from Anastasia and out the window at the swirling snow.

One thing he knew for certain: The Russian people were not happy. Not at all.

❋

Lights illuminated the dark winter night for blocks around the Winter Palace the evening of the ball.

Like everything in the Tsar's regimented world, the ball began at exactly eight thirty.

At the other formal parties and balls, Maisie had been happy to wear the velvet and lace dresses Great-Uncle Thorne had packed for her. But even those didn't compare to this gorgeous one made for her by the Imperial seamstress. Maisie, in her beautiful white-and-silver dress, her hair upswept and held with the diamond barrette, stood at the top of the white marble State Gala Staircase with its red velvet carpet. Above it hung a gigantic gold-and-crystal chandelier. Sculptures, paintings, marble, and mirrors lined the staircase, and Maisie recognized more than one painting with Leonardo da Vinci's signature on it.

The ceilings in every room reached skyward, higher than any Maisie had ever seen anywhere.

She felt dwarfed here, a small speck of a girl in a fancy dress.

But her dress paled in comparison to the gowns the women ascending the staircase now wore. Their jewels glistened in the light, like millions of fireflies were escorting them inside.

Palm trees lined the corridor leading to the

ballroom. Two different types of troopers stood at attention along the vast corridor: one kind wore all white with shiny silver helmets. The others wore bright red.

Felix and Anastasia joined Maisie and watched the people climbing the State Gala Staircase.

"How many people are coming, anyway?" Maisie finally asked.

"Three thousand," Anastasia said simply.

"Three thousand?" Maisie blurted.

Anastasia nodded. "It's an Imperial ball, after all," she said.

"Who are those guys in the tight fur pants?" Maisie asked.

"Hussar soldiers," Anastasia said. "It takes two men to pull those on."

Suddenly, a man in a black-and-gold uniform appeared. He held a walking stick like Great-Uncle Thorne used. His was black and topped with an enormous gold double-headed eagle.

The man tapped his stick three times, and everyone grew silent.

"Their Imperial Majesties!" the man announced.

Enormous doors decorated with gold opened,

and all the women bent their knees and dropped their heads.

There sat Nicholas and Alexandra on giant thrones, wearing enormous jeweled crowns, like a king and queen in a fairy tale.

The orchestra began to play, and soon the guests were waltzing past Maisie, Felix, and Anastasia.

One of the Hussar soldiers asked Maisie to dance, and before she could decline, he had one hand on her waist and the other was holding hers high. He swirled her away from Felix and Anastasia.

"Is it true," Maisie asked him, "that it takes two men to pull those pants on?"

The soldier laughed.

"Yes! It is true!" he said.

Anastasia led Felix outside to a balcony overlooking the gardens, though they were snow-covered, with high drifts and icicles.

"I wish you never had to go back to America," Anastasia said.

In the moonlight, she looks beautiful, Felix thought. He felt a tug of something. Something pulling him home, back to Newport and Elm Medona. But he felt the tug of something else, something pulling for him to stay. Was Alex Andropov right? Could they escape in January 1917? Or even sooner? Could he take Anastasia with him, and save her life?

"You look so serious," Anastasia said, placing one hand on Felix's cheek.

"I was just thinking about how much I would like to stay here," he said, his throat feeling suddenly dry.

Inside, the orchestra had stopped.

The man who had called everyone to attention was tapping his staff again.

"Oh," Anastasia said, disappointed, "we need to go inside."

"Why?" Felix asked, also disappointed.

"He's going to introduce the special guest from America," she said, taking Felix's hand and leading him back inside.

Everyone was silent.

The man announced:

"Ladies and gentlemen! We present to you Mr. Phinneas Pickworth!"

CHAPTER TWELVE

THE END

Maisie gasped. There, right in front of her, was her great-great-grandfather, the very man who had created The Treasure Chest. If only Great-Uncle Thorne had hidden in the chest like Alexander Andropov thought to do, he would be standing face-to-face with his father right now.

Beside Tsar Nicholas and Tsarina Alexandra stood a giant of a man. Six feet six, with a shiny bald head and eyes so blue that even from this distance Maisie could make out their color. His face was craggy, as if he'd spent a lot of time at sea. Tanned and handsome, he towered over the Tsar and Tsarina.

Maisie searched the crowd for a glimpse of Felix. She needed to find her brother, to stare up at their great-great-grandfather with him.

But there were too many people for her to find him.

"Greetings, our esteemed guests," the Tsar announced, "Phinneas Pickworth is a diplomat, an explorer, a gentleman, a citizen of the world. He is here in St. Petersburg to begin his visit to our glorious country of Russia!"

Applause rang through the crowd.

"And Mr. Pickworth would like to address you all," the Tsar said, grasping Phinneas's large hand in his own.

Again the crowd applauded.

When the applause died down, Phinneas looked down at everyone.

"Ladies and gentlemen," he said. "I have traveled the globe. From the tombs of Egypt to the viaducts of Rome, from the Amazon River to the Himalayas, from Madagascar to Mozambique, I travel the world to learn how to live."

The silence in the room grew thick, as every person, all three thousand guests, listened to Phinneas Pickworth speak. He did not boom like Great-Uncle Thorne. Instead, he spoke in a low, gentle voice that commanded attention.

"Recently," he went on, "I brought a sarcophagus back from the Valley of the Kings, to my home in America."

He paused and glanced at the high ceilings and marble columns.

"In America," he added with a slight smile, "my home, Elm Medona, is considered a mansion. An enormous house. But this palace makes it seem like a mere grain of rice in comparison."

The crowd laughed.

"I brought a sarcophagus there, to Elm Medona, and had a party to open it. We ate and drank and danced in the ballroom, much like you are doing tonight. And then we went into the room where I'd placed the sarcophagus, a hidden room at the top of a staircase hidden behind a magical wall. Press the right spot on the wall, and it opens, revealing the staircase."

He paused.

All eyes were gazing at him.

Except Maisie's.

She was still desperately searching for her brother.

"The sarcophagus was made of alabaster, pure

white, and carved with hieroglyphs. I broke the seal. I opened the lid."

A woman gasped.

"And inside it . . ."

Here he paused again.

The entire crowd seemed to lean forward.

"Another coffin. And inside that one, another. And inside that one, another. Much like your nesting dolls here in Russia."

Everyone smiled.

"Except, finally, when we opened the last coffin, there was the mummy of a pharaoh. Of a man who had once ruled. Here he lay, wrapped in linen, amulets on his body, a grimace on his face."

Phinneas Pickworth dabbed the corners of his eyes.

"In that moment, I realized that history can teach us lessons, my friends. Lessons on how to live better, how to be better. And I promised myself, and my children, that the Pickworths would do just that. We would travel through time, if need be—"

And here Maisie would have sworn he looked right at her.

And then at someone across the room.

Maisie followed Phinneas Pickworth's gaze, and saw that it landed on Felix.

"Excuse me," she said, again and again as she pushed her way through the crowd toward him.

"—to learn the lessons history had for us. What would Leonardo da Vinci, or Alexander Graham Bell, or Julius Caesar, or King Tut tell us if they could? They would tell us simple things. To love each other. To listen to what our elders have to say. To be kind to each other."

The lessons Phinneas Pickworth spoke, Maisie realized, were the very ones that had been given to Felix and her.

She had almost reached Felix when Phinneas said, "They would remind us that our families are everything to us."

"Felix!" Maisie called.

Felix turned toward her.

"I have spent my life acquiring pieces of history," Phinneas Pickworth was saying. "And I say now to you all, that Russia is at a crossroads. Tread carefully, dear, dear people. Love each other!"

"Felix!" Maisie said. "What should we do?"

The Tsar had stood again, and he was thanking

Phinneas Pickworth and wishing him safe journeys.

"The Tsarina and I have asked our Imperial jeweler, Carl Fabergé, to create one of his famous eggs just for you. Now I know that you have purchased others from him, for your late wife, Ariane, and your children. We want to give you yet another, one that we believe will delight you, Mr. Pickworth."

To Maisie and Felix's utter surprise, Jim Hercules appeared, holding their egg on a silver tray.

"The egg!" a voice shouted.

That voice belonged to Alexander Andropov, who burst through the crowd, charging toward the dais.

Phinneas Pickworth had opened the egg and found the surprise of the Pickworth peacock there.

But Felix and Maisie had stopped watching him. Instead, they ran after Alex.

"What in the world . . . ?" the Tsarina asked, peering into the crowd at the three running children.

Now Anastasia joined them.

"I need that egg!" Alex shouted.

"Don't give it to him!" Maisie screamed.

Felix saw the confused look on the Tsar's face,

the wide eyes of the Tsarina, and . . .

And the big smile on Phinneas Pickworth.

He gave Felix and Maisie a slight nod, just as Alex *dove* at him, knocking him off balance and sending the egg flying into the air.

"Oh no!" Felix groaned.

The egg, with its glistening jewels, tumbled once in the air.

Then tumbled again, each time getting closer to crashing onto the marble floor.

Eight hands reached out to catch it before it landed.

But two actually did. The right two: Anastasia's.

Felix let out a cry.

Phinneas Pickworth said, "Well done!"

Maisie sighed with relief.

And then Maisie and Felix lifted off the ground, and they, too, began to tumble toward home.

Soon, they would be back in Elm Medona telling Great-Uncle Thorne all about what had happened to them and who they had met in Imperial Russia. He would weep when he heard their story—with joy and wonder that somehow the Pickworth Paradoxia Perpetuity made it possible for his beloved father to appear, and for history to carry on, even as the modern world continued to move forward.

But in this instant, Alexander Andropov, much to Maisie and Felix's surprise—and Alex's—was firmly on the ground there in Russia in 1911.

Phinneas Pickworth smiled up at them.

Anastasia's upturned face was twisted in sadness, the egg clutched tightly in her hands.

Felix tried to stop it all, tried to keep from leaving even as he realized it was impossible. They had not done what the message asked them to do. They had not helped Anastasia, or any of the royal family.

"Felix!" she called, her voice already distant.

With all his might, he shouted, "Anastasia! Don't worry! I'll be back!"

Anastasia shouted something in reply.

But it was too late.

Maisie and Felix were home.

GRAND DUCHESS ANASTASIA NIKOLAEVNA ROMANOV

June 18, 1901—July 17, 1918

In Imperial Russia, as with most monarchies, it was important to have a son to be the heir to the throne. Anastasia was the fourth daughter born to Tsar Nicholas II and his wife, Tsarina Alexandra. Her older sisters were the Grand Duchesses Olga, Tatiana, and Maria. When the Tsar learned that his wife had given birth to yet another daughter, he was so disappointed that he went for a long walk rather than rush to see her. In honor of Anastasia's birth, her father pardoned and reinstated students who had been imprisoned for demonstrating in the capital months earlier. The name *Anastasia* means "the prisoner opener." Three years later, her brother, Alexei, was born to great celebration across Russia.

Despite the vast wealth of the Tsar of Russia, Nicholas believed in a spartan lifestyle. His daughters all slept in one room, on hard cots without blankets, took cold baths, and had household chores as well as community service. He was a reluctant heir to the throne, preferring travel and society to more serious matters. Nicholas's father, Tsar Alexander III, was a powerful man, so strong that he could bend iron pokers with his bare hands. He began every day by going into the woods to hunt. Alexander III believed that true Russians were simple in every way, and it was this philosophy that shaped his son's household as well.

Although Alexander III was considered a progressive ruler by some, during his thirteen-year reign he maintained full control of Russia. There was no parliament and no voting by Russian citizens. He had complete control over every decision, the army and navy, and every citizen. This kind of control is called an *autocracy*, and Alexander III devoted much of his energy as Tsar to crushing opposition to this idea of governing. When he died suddenly in 1894 at the age of forty-nine, his son became Tsar at a time when unrest was spreading throughout Russia. Lacking the strength of his father, Nicholas was unable to keep control of his throne and his country as his father had.

By 1901, when Anastasia was born, protests by workers, farmers, students, and ethnic minorities were erupting. In 1905, the massacre of nearly one thousand unarmed protestors at the Winter Palace, called Bloody Sunday, led to a formation of parliament as well as other concessions by the Tsar. But most of these agreements were on paper only, and Nicholas still maintained complete control of Russia.

The Tsarina Alexandra was also blamed in part for the lack of trust that Russians developed for their monarchy. Her predecessor, Alexander's wife, Marie, was beloved by everyone. Born Princess Dagmar of Denmark, Marie charmed everyone she met. She loved parties and dancing and was embraced by the Russian people as a role model. In contrast, Alexandra was considered cold and aloof, and she alienated her subjects by keeping to herself and presenting a stern face in public. However, it is believed that part of her isolation was to keep her son, Alexei, safe.

Alexei was born with hemophilia, an inability to clot blood that is inherited through the mother (sometimes called the royal disease because it afflicted royal families in Spain, Great Britain, and Russia). Alexandra could trace her genetic connection to her grandmother, Queen Victoria of England, whose youngest son, Leopold, had the disease and died at the age of thirty-one. A year before Alexei was born, Alexandra's four-year-old nephew, Prince Henry of Prussia, died from bleeding. It's no wonder that Alexandra became overly protective of her own son. But because the royal family hid their son's illness from the public, her behavior was judged as insulting.

Anastasia and her sisters led a charmed life despite their brother's illness. They had private tutors, attentive parents, and most of all, each other. The four Grand Duchesses played only with each other, calling themselves OTMA (for Olga, Tatiana, Maria, and Anastasia) as a sign of their closeness and solidarity. Together they swam and hiked, ice-skated and sledded, studied their lessons, put on skits, and entertained each other and their parents and brother.

Because Anastasia died so young, at the age of seventeen, little is known about her. We do know that she was the naughty sister, known to go under the table and bite the legs of guests at royal dinners. She was an excellent mimic, and her imitations, though mocking, were also funny and very accurate. A tomboy, she loved to climb trees, run, swim, and skate. Olga was known as the shy, smart one; Tatiana, the talented, opinionated one; Maria, the beautiful one; and Anastasia, the clown.

By 1917, the Russian Revolution was spreading quickly across the country, from Petrograd to St. Petersburg, and citizens stormed the freezing cold streets, demanding bread. At 3:00 PM on March 15,

1917, on the advice of his generals, Nicholas II abdicated his throne. The royal family was put under house arrest at the Alexander Palace in Tsarskoe Selo. Eventually, they were moved to Siberia, and then when the Bolsheviks seized control of Russia, moved again to Ekaterinburg. The Grand Duchesses, hoping to escape, sewed jewels into their clothing.

Russia quickly broke out in civil war, and negotiations by other royal families of Europe with the Bolsheviks to free the Romanovs ended. The civil war was between the Reds—the Bolsheviks—and the Whites, who were anti-Bolshevik, though not necessarily pro-Tsar. When the Whites arrived at Ekaterinburg, the royal family was gone, and assumed to have been murdered. It was not until 1989 that an accurate account of Anastasia and her family's last hours was revealed.

The family was awakened in the middle of the night and told to dress so that they could be moved to a new, safer location. Instead of leaving, they were brought into the basement and told that they were going to be executed. Then the bodies were burned and buried in a mass grave. The murders were so terrible that for many years, despite an official announcement about the murders, people debated if the family had really been executed. But in 1991, their grave was found.

In 1991, the family was given a state funeral, followed by a ceremony of Christian burial seven years later. The bodies were laid to rest with the other monarchs dating back to Peter the Great in the St. Catherine Chapel in the Peter and Paul cathedral in St. Petersburg. President Boris Yeltsin attended the funeral. The Russian Orthodox Church praised the family for their humbleness, patience, and meekness. And in 2008, the Russian Supreme Court ruled that Nicholas II and his entire family were victims of political repression. Although nothing can diminish the horror of the fate of the Romanovs, history, Russia, and the Russian Orthodox Church have made reparations, giving the Romanovs the honor and dignity they deserved.

Rasputin
January 21, 1869—December 29, 1916

Rasputin is one of the most controversial figures in Russian history, if not in world history. How did a man who never bathed, who had little formal schooling and no manners, who was called "the mad monk" or "the devil Rasputin," gain the confidence and trust of the royal family? Born into a peasant family in Siberia, he was said to have the gift of prophecy at an early age. He arrived in St. Petersburg in 1906 and quickly got a reputation as a healer and a mystic. A year later, he was called upon to help the young Tsarevich, Alexei, when he suffered from a severe hemorrhage due to his hemophilia. When Rasputin seemingly cured the boy, he won his way into the hearts of the family, and in particular, Empress Alexandra. As time went on, politicians, journalists, and the Russian people grew suspicious of Rasputin and his influence over the royal family. People tried to warn the Empress about public opinion toward Rasputin, but she remained his strongest defender. On December 29, 1916, political rivals of Tsar Nicholas II kidnapped and murdered Rasputin. Although the strength of his influence over the Tsar and Tsarina is debatable (some claim that his only purpose in their lives was to keep Alexei healthy; others believe he hypnotized Alexandra and used his power over her politically), historians agree that his presence in the royal family and his closeness to Empress Alexandra added to growing negative feelings toward them. To this day, people debate this mysterious man. Some consider him a mystic; others a mad man.

ANN HOOD

I do so much research for each book in The Treasure Chest series and discover so many cool facts that I can't fit into every book. Here are some of my favorites from my research for *The Treasure Chest: #10: Anastasia Romanov: The Last Grand Duchess.* Enjoy!

When I was in elementary school, there was a television show called *Saturday Afternoon at the Movies.* It showed old black-and-white movies from the 1940s and 1950s, often two or three in a row. Back then, there was no Netflix or On Demand—the only way to watch older movies was when they played on TV. On Sundays and late at night, you could often find an old movie playing. Since there were only three television stations—and no cable!—our choices were limited on what to watch. As a result, I ended up seeing a lot of old movies a lot of times!

Every Saturday afternoon (big surprise!), my grandmother Mama Rose and I would watch *Saturday Afternoon at the Movies.* One of my favorites to show up there was a 1956 film called *Anastasia*. It starred the actress Ingrid Bergman as a woman with amnesia who bears a remarkable resemblance to Grand Duchess Anastasia.

I didn't know then that ever since the massacre of the royal family in 1918, a rumor had persisted that Anastasia had survived and escaped. I also didn't know that for years many women had claimed to be the real Anastasia. Allegedly, the Romanov fortune is in a bank vault somewhere in Europe waiting to be claimed. Perhaps that rumor led to so many Anastasia imposters. Her Aunt Olga, Nicholas's sister, had to endure meeting many of these women in the years following the massacre. After speaking to them she easily debunked their claims.

However, that old movie *Anastasia* never answered the question of whether or not the woman played by Ingrid Bergman was the real Anastasia. Instead, it left it up to the viewer to decide. If you were a nine-year-old girl with an active imagination, living in a small town—like me!—it was easy to believe that Anastasia had survived. Easier to believe that than to accept the harsh truth of what happened to the royal family. Plus, I loved a mystery (still do!). I had read all the Nancy

Drew books by then, and the mystery of Anastasia, with its tragic backstory and intrigue of amnesia and escape, appealed to me.

Among the many Anastasia imposters, one stood out as the most likely person to be the Grand Duchess, had she managed to survive. When I was in middle school, I read a newspaper article about a woman named Anna Anderson. The title was something like: "Is This Woman the Real Grand Duchess Anastasia?" The blurry black-and-white photo that ran with the article looked, to me, very much like Anastasia, whose photograph appeared beside Anna Anderson's. I loved the idea that Anastasia had survived! And over the years, I followed the story of Anna Anderson with great interest.

Anna Anderson was first thought to be one of the Grand Duchesses in 1922. Two years earlier, she had attempted to jump off a bridge in Berlin. When she was rescued by police, she refused to show her identification papers or to reveal her name. The police brought her to a hospital, where they discovered she had many scars on her head and body, typical of a violent attack. Another patient there believed the woman was Grand Duchess Tatiana, and upon her release from the hospital told a Russian friend that she had met Tatiana Romanov. A series of Russians who had known the royal family traveled to Berlin to meet the woman. One of them declared with certainty, "She is too short to be Tatiana." To which the woman replied, "I never said I was Tatiana."

A nurse at the hospital said that the woman had confided to her that she was Grand Duchess Anastasia, but that she suffered amnesia. After her release, she took the name Anna—a nickname for Anastasia. When she became very ill and near death in 1924, many Russians, including the Grand Duchesses' tutor, the Tsar's sister Olga, and Anastasia's nursemaid, all visited her in the hospital and all believed she was *not* Anastasia.

She survived her illness, and an informal investigation into her identity began. Although other friends and family members concluded she was the Grand Duchess, another story about her identity surfaced. That story said she was a Polish factory worker who was badly injured in an explosion and had disappeared from Berlin, Germany, in 1920—the year Anna appeared on the bridge there. When the Dowager Empress Marie, Nicholas's mother, died in 1928, a dozen living relatives of the Tsar's signed a declaration that Anna was a fraud.

Still, the belief persisted that she was Grand Duchess Anastasia. She took the name Anna Anderson and her papers used the details of Anastasia's life. Staunch supporters of her identity in Germany and the United States supported her, let her live with them, and fought to verify that she was indeed Anastasia, just as disbelievers fought to debunk her.

Eventually, in 1968, Anna Anderson moved to Charlottesville, Virginia, where she married Jack Manahan, who called himself a Grand Duke-in-waiting. A year later, lawsuits from both sides ended without a resolution as to her true identity. Until her death in 1984, Anna Anderson never let up on her claim that she was Grand Duchess Anastasia Romanov.

In 1919, the White government in Russia began an investigation into the massacre of the royal family. The mass grave was found in 1991, and with it many personal items, such as the Tsar's belt buckle, the Tsarina's pearl earring, the Grand Duchesses' shoe buckles, and many, many charred bones. With modern advances in technology, the technique of identifying people through DNA analysis has become a useful investigative tool. In 1991, the bones from the mass grave were identified through DNA analysis as those of Tsar Nicholas, Tsarina Alexandra, and three of their daughters. Rather than settle the question of whether Anastasia had survived, this discovery fueled a new round of speculation. If only three Grand Duchesses' bodies could be accounted for, wasn't it possible Anastasia, the fourth Grand Duchess, had escaped?

However, as science continued to develop more refined techniques, a new round of DNA testing was done on the bones from the mass grave in Ekaterinburg in 2007. This time, DNA tests confirmed the identity of Alexei and Anastasia, too. In addition, DNA testing was done on a lock of Anna Anderson's hair. Those tests proved she was not a Romanov—she was the Polish factory worker, Franziska Schanzkowska.

For me, this nearly definitive evidence proves that Anastasia perished with the rest of her family on that terrible July night in 1918. How I wish she had survived! The idea of Anastasia escaping the massacre represented a kind of hope for me as a little girl, and for many other people who wanted to believe that despite this bloody chapter in history, at least one little girl had been saved.

About the Author

Ann Hood is the author of many books, including *How I Saved My Father's Life (and Ruined Everything Else)*. She also knits, wanders around museums, wears cool glasses, likes to play on her iPhone, and spends a lot of her time wishing she could time travel and meet famous people.